Sassy

The Silver Secret

Sharon M. Draper

SCHOLASTIC PRESS
New York

This book is dedicated
with much love
to Anthony James Christian Colts,
who loves music and rhythm and song

Library of Congress Cataloging-in-Publication Data Available

ISBN 978-0-545-07153-6

10 9 8 7 6 5 4 3 2 1   10 11 12 13 14

Printed in the U.S.A.   23
First edition, May 2010

Book design by Elizabeth B. Parisi

CHAPTER ONE

Sassy's Silver Secret

"I've got a big, huge secret!" I whisper to my friend Jasmine.

We are sitting on my sofa, eating popcorn and watching a movie we've seen seventeen times.

We quote the lines along with the characters.

We know every single word of all the songs.

We even sing the songs together, sort of.

Well, Jasmine sings. I croak. My singing voice sounds like a hyena in pain. Pretty ugly.

"So tell me!" Jasmine pleads. She never takes her eyes from the screen. It's almost time for the next song.

"I can't," I explain. "It's a secret!"

"Is it a good one or a bad one?" she asks.

"Oooh, absolutely the best." I giggle a little as I think about it.

"I can't wait to hear it!" she says. She turns her head to look at me.

"I can't tell you!" I say with frustration.

She tosses some popcorn at my head. "So why did you even mention it?"

"Because I think I'll explode if I don't tell somebody, and you're my best friend."

"I'd hate for you to blow up. What's the secret?"

"I can't say. Not yet."

"Why not?"

"It's complicated," I tell her with a sigh.

Jasmine and I share everything. Green, glittery nail polish. Orange bangle bracelets. Stickers with hearts and flowers. Shoes. And secrets. Well, most of the time. I feel bad I can't tell her yet.

The television screen fills with the kids in the movie. It's time for "The Moonlight and Peppermint Song." Jasmine, whose voice is a silvery soprano just like the cute teenage girl who has the lead in the film, begins to sing.

"Moonlight brings magic . . ." she begins.

I join in loudly. *". . . to all peppermint dreams. . . ."* I must be part screech owl.

"Stop, Sassy!" Jasmine says with a laugh. "Your voice makes me need earmuffs!"

"I know. I know," I admit. "I love music. It's not fair I can't sing."

"Let's just listen to the kids in the movie, okay?" Jasmine says. She continues to sing with the music in the film. Even though I know all the words, I don't even hum. Somebody might think a cow got loose in our house if I hummed along.

The good-looking guy and the attractive girl end up singing happily in the moonlight, dreaming of peppermints and romance. The movie credits roll as the instrumental versions of all the songs are repeated.

Jasmine asks me, "Do you want to watch it again?"

"Not right now," I tell her. "You want a piece of candy?"

"Like, do you have to ask?" she says as she holds out her hand. "I know you've got candy and glitter and stickers and probably a million other things stuffed down in that purse of yours."

"Maybe two million," I tell her with a grin. I carry what I call my Sassy Sack every single day — my wonderful, glorious, beautifully shiny shoulder bag. It's purple and silver and pink and magenta. It has a long strap, several outside compartments with buttons and zippers, and lots of little hidden pockets inside.

There are diamond-looking sparkly things all over it, and

when I'm outside and the sunlight hits it just right, it really shines.

Even I'm not sure of all that's in there, but I know when I reach down into it, I always seem to find exactly what I need.

I dig into my Sassy Sack and pull out two Jolly Rancher candies — both grape.

"Purple, of course!" Jasmine says.

"My favorite color and flavor," I answer as I pop the unwrapped candy into my mouth at the same time she does.

"Yum!" we say together.

"So you're not going to tell me your secret?" Jasmine asks once more.

"I can't. Not yet," I tell her.

"That is *so* not fair!" she says, sounding a little annoyed with me.

I don't blame her. I've never kept a secret from her — especially something this cool.

"I can tell you this much," I say. "It's about the choir. I've got to find a way to be in the show."

"Sassy, you're my BFF, but face it — you're not the best singer in the world. To tell the truth — you're probably the worst singer on the planet!"

We both laugh.

Just then my twelve-year-old brother, Sabin, comes into the living room, grabs the remote, and switches the television to the sports channel.

"Sabin!" we both cry out. "We were here first!"

"Aw, quit complaining," he says. "Your movie is over. I heard you two giggling at the love scenes."

"We were not!" Jasmine declares. But we both know he's telling the truth.

Sabin continues. "I also heard you trying to sing with the music. Sassy, I think you broke my ears!"

We both throw sofa pillows at him, but he just laughs, ducks, and turns up the volume on the basketball game.

I grab my Sassy Sack, Jasmine takes the rest of the popcorn, and we head upstairs to my room. I love my room. It's messy but classy. I have a pale lavender bedspread, matching curtains, and rose-colored walls. The carpet is ugly and brown. I can't do much about that, so Mom bought me pink-and-purple throw rugs to cover it up. They help — a little.

Jasmine flops onto my bed. "Let's do our nails!" she suggests.

On my desk I have seven different colors of sparkly nail polish. In my Sassy Sack I keep three more — just in case I need to do my nails in the car or at the mall.

"Great idea. What color?" I ask her.

"Silver!" she says. "Doesn't the word *silver* sound special and shiny?"

That's why Jasmine is my best friend. We think alike.

"My secret is silver," I whisper.

Jasmine gasps. "Come on, Sassy! Quit teasing. You gotta tell me!"

"I will," I promise her. "As soon as I can."

She doesn't seem satisfied, but she seems to believe me.

I pull the silver glitter polish from my Sassy Sack. We talk softly as we take turns carefully painting each other's fingernails and toenails.

"Does the secret have something to do with silver nail polish?" she asks.

"No."

"Silver candy wrappers?"

"Nice, but no."

"Silver house paint?"

"That's crazy!"

"A silver car?"

"I wish!"

"Silver glitter glue?"

"Nope!"

"Sassy, you're driving me crazy! Tell me, please!"

"Well," I begin.

Then my sixteen-year-old sister, Sadora, comes into my room. She's pretty as a model, can sing like a nightingale, and almost *always* gets the lead in the plays at her school. Our whole family goes to every single performance and cheers her on.

"Did you borrow my red nail polish, Little Sister?" she asks.

Sometimes my family calls me by my nickname, Little Sister, and sometimes they call me Sassy. I like it so much better when they call me by my real name.

"Your red polish is in the bathroom," I tell her. "It was all dried up and yucky, so I didn't touch it."

She sighs. "Well, can I borrow your red sparkly polish, Sassy? I see you and Jasmine are into silver today."

"Okay," I say, "but be sure to put the top back on real tight when you're done!" I reach into my Sassy Sack, pull out a brand-new bottle of Romantic Red, and hand it to her slowly.

She grabs it and hurries out of my room.

"I wish I had an older sister," Jasmine says. "I just have a little brother."

"Be glad you're older," I tell her. "Most of the time I'm invisible around here. Usually Sadora doesn't even ask to borrow my stuff — she just grabs what she needs. Sometimes she forgets to return it."

"Yeah, but she's sixteen. She must know *everything* about teachers and boys and parents and stuff!" Jasmine's voice sounds wishful.

"It's possible," I tell Jasmine, "but she's never told me any of that."

We add a second coat of silver polish.

"Silver," Jasmine says softly. "I wish I had a silver secret. If I did, I would tell my best friend and not drive her crazy."

"I'm not trying to be mean, Jasmine. Honest. And when you find out what it is, you'll be real happy for me."

Jasmine grins. "Okay, you win. But you have to tell me soon, okay?"

"Okay." We hook our pinkies together and promise. We are careful not to smear the fresh polish.

"You know the tryouts for the musical are held after school tomorrow," Jasmine says. "So I won't be riding home on the bus with you. My mom is going to pick me up."

"Uh, I might stick around and watch," I say real casually.

"Okay. My mom can take us both home, then," she says.

"So," I say as we are waiting for our nails to dry, "when Mr. Wood calls people onstage for tryouts, what part do you want?"

Jasmine smiles. "I'd love to sing the ocean song. It makes

me think about the wind blowing on the sails of a boat when we sing it in class."

"You'd be great for that part," I tell her honestly.

"But what about you, Sassy? Won't you get tired just sitting there listening to other people sing?"

"I want to watch the tryouts because maybe I can figure out a way to be in the show."

"Doing what? And how does this figure into the silver secret that you won't tell me about?" She's getting upset again.

"I'm not sure yet, but there's got to be *something* I can do so I can be onstage."

"What about your secret?" Jasmine asks.

"It's cool, but I don't think it will get me a part in the musical," I tell her sadly.

"So when are you going to tell me?"

"Soon," I say. "I promise."

Just then Sabin's dog trots into my room.

"Sabin! Come and get Zero! He smells like old fish!" I cry.

A brown beagle jumps up on my bed and smears the silver polish on my little finger.

"Sabin! Hurry! He's messing up my nail polish!"

"When did Sabin get a dog?" Jasmine asks. She jumps up so her nails are out of the dog's way.

"A couple of weeks ago. Sabin's friend Raphael moved to New York. His family is living in an apartment and he couldn't keep the dog. So my brother begged Mom and Daddy to let him adopt Zero."

"Zero?"

"Yep. I think that's his IQ score. I've never seen a goofier animal."

"Your parents actually agreed to let Sabin have a dog? Parents always say no to that kind of stuff."

"I know. Mom and Dad told Sabin they'd give him a month to see if he does what he promised about feeding Zero and taking him outside."

"What about bathing him?" Jasmine covers her nose.

"Dream on." I fix my polish while the dog sniffs under my bed.

"Haven't you been asking for a cocker spaniel since your last birthday?"

"I sure have. But Daddy says Zero will be the family dog if he fits in. That's just so not fair!"

Sabin rushes into my room. "C'mon, Zero! It's time for your bath!"

The dog bounds out with an old pink sock in his mouth. He runs down the hall as if he understands what Sabin said.

"Come back, Zero!" Sabin calls after him.

"Maybe he's not so stupid after all!" Jasmine says with a laugh.

"Oh, yes he is. He eats socks."

"Huh?"

"You know how socks always get lost in the wash?"

"Yeah."

"Well, ever since that dog got here, we don't have that problem. Zero eats them before they have a chance to get lost."

"That's the funniest thing I ever heard!"

"I've watched him do it. He starts at the toe, then unravels it and pulls it apart and gobbles it a chunk at a time."

"What else does he eat?"

"Besides socks? None of that dry brown food my mother buys. He likes fruits and veggies. Stuff like broccoli, lemons, onions, and tomatoes."

Jasmine is rolling on the floor with laughter.

"And then, of course, he throws up."

"Oh, yuck!"

"Yesterday Zero threw up in the living room. Blue socks and green peas and red pizza sauce."

"Disgusting!"

"Yep, a multicolor mess. Zero ran and hid under the sofa. And Sabin had to clean it up!"

Jasmine is holding herself, giggling uncontrollably. "Has

the dog eaten anything silver?" she asks. "Maybe that's your silver secret."

"Not hardly," I reply with a smile. "My secret is super special. It's going to make me shine!"

Jasmine is still laughing when her mother comes to pick her up.

"I'll see you tomorrow at school, Sassy," she says, wiping tears from her eyes. "And I'm not going to let you keep that secret much longer!"

CHAPTER TWO

Just Hum, Sassy

We have choir the last period of the day. The choir room is really just a small classroom with the chairs pushed to the wall. The risers we stand on are ancient and wobbly.

Everybody in fourth grade takes choir, even if they can't sing. We don't have an orchestra. Mr. Wood, our music teacher, would love to have one, I think. But he says our school doesn't have enough money to buy instruments.

So Mr. Wood has to listen to us sing. All of us. Carmelita probably has the most powerful soprano in the school. Even Travis, who once got his head stuck in a chair, has a strong tenor voice. Jasmine could probably make it on one of those singing-contest shows on television.

Me? I croak. I gobble. I squeak.

Mr. Wood says to me, "Just hum, Sassy, and enjoy the music."

That's a nice way of saying, "Sassy, keep your mouth shut. If you sing, your voice might trigger the fire alarm and we'd never learn the song!"

So I stand on the risers with everyone else. I learn the words and the music to every song, but I don't sing. I don't really mind. I know how bad I sound.

Today, however, everybody is excited about the tryouts for the musical.

"Do we get to wear costumes?" Jasmine asks as soon as class starts.

"Yes, indeed!" Mr. Wood replies. His body is round like a drum. Even his head is round and bald. When he laughs, his voice sounds like deep bass music.

"What kind of costumes?" Holly asks.

Mr. Wood goes over to his desk and picks up two large blue packages.

"Listen up, children. Instead of our usual singing class today, let's talk about the upcoming show, the tryouts, and all that goes with it."

Everybody cheers at that, and we take our seats instead of standing on the risers.

"Hey, Sassy," Holly whispers as we sit down. "Do you have a nail file? I broke my fingernail and I keep scratching myself!"

"Sure, Holly," I whisper back. I reach down into my Sassy

Sack, pull out a pink emery board decorated with flowers, and hand it to her.

"Thanks!" She quickly fixes her nail and hands the emery board back to me.

Mr. Wood clears his throat to let us know he wants us to be quiet. "This is the first time I've attempted to do such a show, but I want to put on something special this year. Even though we don't have an orchestra, I think we can have a very fine musical."

"What will we use for background music?" Travis asks.

"I've got five thousand songs on my iPod!" Mr. Wood responds with a chuckle.

"I bet you have nothing but oldies!" Rusty says, teasing.

"The older the better!" Mr. Wood tells him.

Rusty and Travis groan.

"You never told us what we would be wearing," Holly reminds him.

Mr. Wood opens the first blue package. "The boys," he begins, "will wear white shirts, dark blue slacks —"

"That sounds like our school uniforms!" Travis complains, interrupting.

"You didn't let me finish," Mr. Wood replies. "They will also wear these vests!" He pulls out a bright purple vest covered with sparkly sequins from the package.

All the girls say, "Ooh, wow! Awesome."

All the boys just say, "Ooh, wow." It's like they aren't sure if they like them or not.

"Try it on, Travis," Mr. Wood suggests.

Travis takes the vest, puts it on over his shirt, and buttons it up. "Hey, man, I look *too* good!" he boasts to Rusty.

Mr. Wood lets Rusty and Clarence and Todd all model the sparkly vests. They strut around the room like they're movie stars or something.

"I really like them," I tell Jasmine.

"For real," she replies.

"What about the girls?" Carmelita asks. "What will we wear?"

Mr. Wood collects the vests, folds them, and tucks them carefully back into the package.

"The girls," Mr. Wood says slowly and with a big grin on his face, "will wear these!"

He opens the second package and pulls out the most beautiful dress I have ever seen in my life. It's a pale purple — absolutely the first on my list of favorite colors. It almost shimmers in the afternoon sunlight that streams through the classroom window. It has purple and silver sequins all over it, a tiny waistline, and a full, twirly skirt. I gasp.

"That is just *too* beautiful," Jasmine gushes.

All the rest of the girls nod in agreement.

"Can I try it on?" Carmelita asks. "Please?"

Mr. Wood checks the tag to see if it's her size, then gives her the dress. Carmelita grabs the hall pass and rushes to the bathroom to try it on.

"That dress sure will make me pretty!" Holly says.

"Me, too," Jasmine adds. "How can you sing ugly when you're wearing an outfit that gorgeous?"

I am quiet and don't say anything. But I know I just *have* to be in that show. One of those dresses is going to be mine!

Carmelita returns wearing the dress. She looks like a princess. She sparkles. She glows. She twirls for us and bows, and then she sings the first line of a song about feeling pretty, just to show how much the dress helps her voice.

She's right. The dress makes her sing even better than she usually does, and Carmelita can throw down a song.

Everybody claps.

She takes a bow and then hurries to change out of the wonderful outfit.

When she gets back, Mr. Wood says to us, "I showed you the costumes so you can know what you'll look like onstage in the show. That was inspiration. Now comes the hard work."

"Work?" Rusty says.

"Yes, it's a hard job to put on a show. We need lots of people to help. Every job is important."

"Can't I just show up and look good?" Travis asks with a grin.

"No, Travis. It's not that easy," Mr. Wood tells him. "Let me explain how the tryouts will go. If you want a featured singing part, you will sing for me after school. I will choose the best voices."

"Will there be dancing parts?" Holly asks. She takes dancing lessons twice a week.

"Yes, Holly, I think there will be a couple of parts for dancers in the show."

"Yay!" She jumps up and does a little ballet twirl on her toes.

"What about people who can't sing or dance?" Rusty asks. I'm glad nobody looks at me when he says it.

Mr. Wood replies cheerfully, "We need people to make the sets and decorate the auditorium. We'll also need ushers and people to operate the curtain. So there will be something important for each person to do."

When the bell rings, instead of packing up and leaving for home, most of the kids go to the auditorium for the tryouts. Our school is real old, and our auditorium is pretty beat-up. It has a thick, dark curtain that rises, but it's got holes in it. I can see where it has been patched and sewn many, many times.

We have real stage lights that glow in different colors, but lots of times they won't come on, or the bulbs are blown out. The auditorium has rows of seats that could use some cushions. The wooden seats sometimes scratch the legs of the people who are sitting in them.

But it's an awesome place anyway. It's always cool and dark and a little mysterious. We only go in there for assemblies, like when my grammy came to do her storytelling show, or for special events like choir performances and sixth-grade graduation.

Mr. Wood sits in the front row and reads names off a sheet in front of him. "We'll start with the singers," he says. "Carmelita!" he calls out.

"I need background music," Carmelita says.

"No problem," Mr. Wood says. "Let me plug my iPod into the player."

He gets up, slips it into the slot, and pushes PLAY. Nothing happens.

"What's up, Mr. Wood?" Carmelita asks.

"Well, it seems we're in a bit of a pickle."

"What do you mean?" asks Travis.

"Well, I left the power plug at home, and the player's battery is dead. Plus, it seems I forgot to charge my iPod last night."

"You're losing it, Mr. Wood," Travis tells him with a smile, "and the show is just getting started!"

"I'm going to need help to keep organized," our teacher answers. "But right now, what are we going to do? Neither the iPod nor the player will work!"

He scratches the top of his bald head.

I reach down into my Sassy Sack and pull out a handful of size C batteries. "Are these the right kind?" I ask him as I walk over to where he is standing.

"You're the best, Sassy!" Mr. Wood says as he plops the batteries into the machine that can now power the iPod. "You've got the most amazing things in that bag of yours. How can I ever thank you? I'll replace these tomorrow — promise."

"That's okay," I say quietly. There's no way I can tell him that he can thank me by letting me be in the show. I go back and sit down in my seat.

The player powers on, the music belts out, and Carmelita sings like a canary. Well, not exactly like a bird, but real pretty. Everybody claps.

"Travis!" Mr. Wood calls next.

Travis runs up to the stage, clears his throat, and blows everybody away with his solo.

"Wow!" Mr. Wood says. "That was powerful!"

"I've been practicing in the shower," Travis replies with a grin.

I've been practicing, too. But I still don't say anything.

Jasmine and Rusty and the other kids all go up and take their turns trying out for singing parts. Mr. Wood does not call my name because I didn't sign up. It would have been a waste of time.

Mr. Wood, like everybody else, does not know my secret. But even I have no idea how my secret will help me get in the show.

When Mr. Wood calls for dancers, lots of kids try out, but I'm sure Holly will get the lead. She moves like water is flowing in her arms and legs.

I don't try out for a dancing part, either. I'm not as bad at dancing as I am at singing, but I'm no Holly. I don't think I'm good enough to dance in the show.

When the tryouts are over, Jasmine's mom comes to pick her up, and she takes me home as well. We usually giggle and make jokes in the car, but I'm still very quiet. Jasmine looks at me funny, but she does not ask about the secret again. When we get to my house, I wave good-bye and hurry up the driveway to my door.

I don't want to be behind the scenes, making sets, or standing at the door, handing out programs. I want to be in the show. I want to be in the spotlight. I *must* wear one of those sparkly dresses.

I want to be a star!

CHAPTER THREE

Dinner, with Piccolo for Dessert!

At dinner, Sabin eats all the dark meat from the chicken platter — as usual. Sadora eats only green beans and carrots — as usual. Sabin rarely eats vegetables and Sadora hardly ever eats meat. I eat whatever Mom cooks. I just hope my family doesn't gobble it all before the platter gets passed around to me.

Daddy is in a good mood, cracking jokes and eating his peas with a knife.

"Sampson, what's got into you?" Mom asks, but she laughs at him anyway. "You're setting a bad example for the children!"

"I'm just showing them how people eat peas on the island of Boo."

"There's no such place," I say to Daddy, giggling a little.

"Yes, there is. I saw it on the Travel Channel. Everyone

on the island of Boo eats their vegetables with a knife. It's a law made by the king."

"You're silly, Daddy," Sadora says.

"When I visited there, they made me champion of the veggie eaters! Nobody could eat more green beans or corn or peas with his knife than me!" He slides a few more vegetables onto his butter knife, then slurps them up.

Sabin, of course, tries to outdo what Daddy does and gobbles mouthfuls of peas and carrots.

Zero sits by Sabin's chair and snatches anything that falls from my brother's plate.

"I can get more peas on my knife than you can, Dad," he boasts.

"Not in a million years!" Daddy replies. "I have a gold medal from the island of Boo to prove it!" He gulps more carrots.

Sabin eats more.

"I beat you, Dad!" Sabin finally says, raising his arms like he's a winner.

"Yes, and I made you eat your vegetables," Daddy says as he picks up his fork.

Sadora and Mom and I crack up. Zero yips as if he understands the joke.

Sabin makes a face. He knows he's been outsmarted.

I check the clock on the wall. "It's almost time, Mom. I don't want to be late for my lesson."

"Okay, honey. Let's go," she says to me. "Sadora, please do the dishes while we're gone, okay?"

She starts to groan, but Daddy gives her a look, so she starts to clear the table.

"And, Sabin, after you walk the dog, don't forget to take out the trash."

"Okay, Mom."

"Don't forget to separate the plastics and stuff for the recycling bin!" I add.

"Now I have to take orders from Sassy, too?" Sabin crosses his arms across his chest.

"Yep. You do," Daddy says in a voice of authority.

I give Daddy a quick hug to thank him, then hurry for the door. I grab my jacket, my instrument, my Sassy Sack, and rush to the car.

Yes, my instrument. I play the piccolo, and nobody knows. Except my family. And I love it.

I'm already sitting in the car with my seat belt on when Mom comes out with her keys. I check my change purse hanging from the key chain on my sack — it's purple and says SASSY on it — simply awesome — to make sure I have enough money to buy a soda when my lesson is over. Blowing that instrument makes me really thirsty.

I also pull out of my sack a small container of breath spray and squirt some into my mouth. I hate to have bad breath. My piccolo teacher, Mrs. Rossini, sometimes gets very close as she is helping me get a section of music just right. She's a nice lady. I'm sure she doesn't want to smell garlic breath for an hour.

"I've listened to you practice upstairs," Mom says as she starts the car. "You're sounding very good these days."

"Mrs. Rossini says I'm really improving," I tell her. "It's getting to be so much *fun* now that I'm past all the baby basic stuff."

"I'm proud of how dedicated you are, Sassy. You've been doing this for over a year now, and not once have you acted like you're ready to quit."

"Quit? No way!" I look out of the window for a minute, then I say to her, "Mom, playing the piccolo is just *me*!"

"How come?" Mom asks.

"Well, it's little like me, and it's got a high voice like me, and it's silvery and shiny. Playing it makes me happy."

Mom smiles at me as we back out of the driveway. "Just like Grammy knew it would," she says with one of those grown-up nods.

My interest in piccolo all started when my grammy took

me and Sabin and Sadora to a concert. Sabin plays the violin in his school orchestra, so he likes that kind of stuff. I thought I would be bored, but the musicians played all kinds of cool songs. One of them had a piccolo solo.

"Is that a flute he's playing?" I had whispered to Grammy. "It's so little!"

"No," she had told me. "It's a piccolo."

"Piccolo. Piccolo. Piccolo," I had repeated over and over. The word still makes me giggle.

"I think the word *piccolo* means 'tiny,'" Grammy had explained.

Just like me, I thought as the concert ended with a crash of cymbals and roar of trumpets.

A few weeks after the concert, a package wrapped in silver paper arrived at my house. I opened it with excitement. It was from Grammy, which is *always* a cool thing.

Inside a black leather case, resting gently on blue velvet, was this perfect silver piccolo, divided into two parts. I carefully slipped the two parts together and held the small treasure in my hands. It was barely a foot long.

A note inside the leather case read, *Let this be your silver secret. Learn to play it, learn to love it. Let its silver melodies always keep you happy. Love, Grammy.*

Mom found a place where I could take lessons, and, even though it was hard at first, I've loved every second of learning to play. Blow gently. Use soft, smooth breaths. Lovely tones come out. The music even *sounds* silvery!

I never told any of the other kids at school — not even Jasmine. Somehow this was something all my own. I didn't want to share it — at least not yet. I was afraid I wouldn't be very good at it.

But it turns out I'm pretty good — actually very good. Mrs. Rossini says she's never seen anyone learn so quickly.

I tell her it's because I love it. She smiles with understanding.

Since we have no orchestra at school, I have never had the chance to perform for anyone on my piccolo.

Plus, all the instrumental music for the upcoming show will come from iPods.

I've thought about it, but I honestly can't figure out how to add piccolo music to our show. It sure would be nice if I could.

But for now, my shiny silver secret has to stay hidden in my Sassy Sack.

CHAPTER FOUR

Stage Manager and Spruce Ups Coming

Just before lunch, Mr. Wood posts the names of the people who will sing in the show. Actually, it's just about everybody who tried out. Carmelita. Travis. Jasmine. Rusty. Ricky. Charles. Abdul. Tandy. Iris. Princess. Misty. Basima. Josephina. Holly gets to dance. Some of the boys are put into trios and will sing and dance, too. Josephina and Jasmine get a duet.

Everybody is excited. Except me. I don't even check the cast list.

Then Jasmine says, "Did you see your name, Sassy?"

"Why should it be there?" I say a little sadly. "I didn't even try out."

"You should check it," Jasmine tells me with a smile.

I walk over to the bulletin board. Mr. Wood has assigned jobs to kids as poster makers and set designers and even ushers. I sigh. Those are nice jobs, but I don't want to do any of that.

I'd love to play my piccolo in the musical, but several things will stop that from happening. First of all, nobody knows I have a piccolo and that I know how to play it. Second, since there are no live instruments in the musical, I'd look pretty stupid showing up with a baby flute.

I guess I kept my secret too well.

I find my name at the very bottom of the list, like maybe Mr. Wood checked it and at the last minute remembered that he had forgotten me.

It says, "Sassy Simone Sanford — stage manager."

Mr. Wood walks over to me then. "You've got class, Sassy. And smarts. And great ideas. I really need your help. You know how forgetful I am. Do you think you can do this job?"

"I think so," I tell him slowly. "What does the stage manager do?"

"She is the one who tells everybody what to do, where to stand, when to come onstage, and when to leave the stage. She tells the curtain puller when to pull it up and when to bring it down. She is in charge."

"Do I get a clipboard?" I ask.

He chuckles. "How about a pink one?"

"Can I wear one of those purple sparkly dresses?" I hold my breath.

"Well," Mr. Wood replies. "I only have enough costumes for the performers who will be on the stage. Most of your work will be done behind the scenes — backstage. But you can wear a pretty outfit — anything you like. And we'll make sure you get to come out and take a bow. How does that sound?"

I sigh, but I agree to do it. He reaches over and shakes my hand. His large hand covers my little one like a giant glove.

"I'll need several pens and markers as well," I tell him. "In lots of different colors. I plan to color coordinate the whole show!"

Mr. Wood laughs his big bass chuckle. "I knew I chose the right person for the job!"

Jasmine asks me then, "Are you happy with the part you got in the show?"

"I like being in charge," I tell her honestly. "But I really want to wear one of those dresses."

"I know," she says, putting her arm around my shoulders. "It's awful you can't wear one. Mr. Wood should have ordered more costumes!"

"He knows I can't sing," I remind her.

"But that's not your fault! This is just so not fair."

I breathe deeply and imagine how I'd look in one of the shimmery dresses. I say, "It's okay." But it really isn't.

"You should get to wear one of those dresses just because you'd look so good in it!" Jasmine tells me.

"Yeah, I would," I admit with a small smile.

Jasmine always knows what to say to make me feel better. We both laugh as we walk down the hall to the cafeteria together.

Sometimes it's hard to find a seat in our lunchroom. Like the rest of our school, the room is old and well-worn. The linoleum floor is scuffed, and in lots of places it's easy to see the bare cement underneath. The tables wobble, but the food is usually pretty good.

"Why does our cafeteria always smell like tomato soup?" Jasmine asks as we enter the hot and crowded room.

"I don't know, because I don't think they've ever even served any kind of soup," I tell her as I crinkle up my nose.

We pick up our disposable trays, get a cheeseburger, a little cup of fruit, and a juice box each, and head to the table where mostly fourth graders are squeezed together.

I like when Travis sits with us. He makes us laugh. He slurps spaghetti and sucks Jell-O cubes into his mouth from the plate. Plus, he's the best milk gargler in the fourth grade.

"Ooh, yuck!" Tandy says. "You've got milk coming out of your nose!"

Travis snorts and does it again. I think he likes to gross us out.

"Give him a tissue, Sassy," Princess says. She knows I keep tissues and bandages and rubber bands down in my Sassy Sack.

I decide my pretty pink tissue is too nice for Travis, so I hand him a brown paper towel instead. He doesn't even notice.

Then Princess looks at the key chain I have hanging on my Sassy Sack. She touches it with admiration and says, "Wow, Sassy. I think you've got the best key chain of all of us!"

"Thanks," I tell her.

All the girls pull out their key chains then. Princess has a small fuzzy stuffed cat, a picture of her baby sister, and a little container full of lip gloss dangling from hers. We all nod with approval.

"I've got miniature ballet shoes, a tiny ballerina doll, and a snood," Holly announces.

"What's a snood?" we ask, giggling because it's a funny word.

"It holds my hair while I dance," she explains.

Jasmine's key chain has hearts and flowers and tiny sunshine charms. Her favorite color is orange.

But mine is the coolest. I've got a tiny pink sparkly book that I can actually write in and three kinds of minishoes — a dressy one with a spiked heel, a sparkly tennis sneaker, and a pink flip-flop that smells like cherries. I've also got a pink dolphin, a heart-shaped charm that says I LOVE PURPLE, two flashlights, some bells on a ribbon, and my change purse that has SASSY written in sparkly letters. And keys. All of us have keys.

"We've got enough keys to drive to Alaska!" I joke.

"And none of us can drive!" Princess cracks up.

"I've got my daddy's car keys from his old car," Holly explains.

"Me, too!" I say. "His new car, too. But I don't think he knows it."

Princess touches my purse gently. "Your Sassy Sack is so cool," she says. "I wish I had one just like it."

"My grammy made it for me," I explain, "so it's one of a kind."

"How did she get all those sparkles and sequins on there?"

"She placed them herself — one at a time. She told me every time she sewed a stitch, she thought of me."

"Awesome," Jasmine whispers.

"What's inside it?" Travis asks, bending his head so he can look inside.

I close the top flap. "Secrets. Specials. Necessaries," I tell him in a whisper.

All of the girls laugh as we glance at each other and nod. We understand.

I'm in a pretty good mood as we return our trays. Being with my friends always makes me feel better.

Our school does a pretty good job of recycling. The disposable cardboard trays, along with glass and plastic juice bottles, go into a big bin with a giant letter R painted on the front. Every classroom has a recycling bin as well. Little stuff like that is important to me.

Just before it is time to go back to class, we hear *bing-bong-bing*. That's the sound that says an announcement is coming over the public address system.

Our principal, Mrs. Bell, has a squeaky voice. When she speaks, it's almost like listening to fingernails on a blackboard.

"Attention, children and teachers," she says. "I have an important announcement that is both good news and bad news." She pauses. "Well, it's not really bad news, but we might have to make some adjustments around here for a few months."

"Maybe they're closing the school for a while," Rusty says with a laugh.

"Not hardly," I tell him.

Mrs. Bell continues. "The good news is that the board of education has finally approved the funds for several improvements to our school. I know it's very crowded around here, and we really need the new space. They are going to spruce up our old building with new floors and new classroom furniture. Plus, they plan to build two new science labs, several new classrooms, and a new music room."

Some of the teachers in the cafeteria stand up and cheer. Mr. Wood is one of them.

Mrs. Bell says then, "The bad news is that construction will start in the next week. Halls will be blocked off, workers will be all over the place making lots of noise, and lots of heavy equipment will fill our parking lot."

Travis and Rusty cheer this time. "Cool, man. Nothing better than a bulldozer!" Travis says.

"Parents will be given notices of all the changes going on in our building. We want you to be safe during this construction and confusion."

Bing-bong-bing. The public address system goes quiet. Then the bell rings and we head for English class with Miss Armstrong.

"I bet she makes us write a poem about all this," Jasmine whispers as we head to class.

"What's poetic about jackhammers and cranes?" I ask.

"Not a thing!" Jasmine replies with a laugh. "Not one single thing!"

CHAPTER FIVE

Construction Woes Decorated with Music

Construction brings lots of noise and confusion and dirt. Huge trucks sometimes block the driveway when parents are dropping their kids off at school. Big wooden planks cover some of the walkways that have been dug up. A large pile of dirt sits in front of the school, and on rainy days everything is covered with brown, yucky mud that gets tracked into the halls and classrooms.

Fairly disgusting.

Today they are installing new plumbing. Because of this, some of the toilets do not flush.

Really disgusting.

Men and women with dirty yellow hard hats sometimes walk down the halls with us. They are supposed to stay on the side where the new area is being built, but sometimes they need to use the phones or the bathrooms. Good luck on that one!

Sometimes they get their lunch from our cafeteria. Why would anybody want to eat our cafeteria food on purpose? I don't get it.

We are not allowed to go anywhere near the construction zone. Barriers and fences have been set up. We can't even get close. But we can watch the progress from a distance, especially when we are outside for recess.

Jasmine, Princess, Holly, Carmelita, and I are sitting on a bench, watching the new building in progress. Lots of other kids have their noses close to the fence that separates the kids from the builders.

"It looks like a giant skeleton," I tell Jasmine. "The boards are skinny like bones, and the nails connect them all together like joints."

"It smells good," Jasmine says as she sniffs the air. "I like the smell of sawdust. It smells so *new*."

"When is all this supposed to be finished?" Holly asks as we watch a crane move stuff from a pile to a truck.

"My father says the new wing of the building should be ready by the time school starts next fall," Jasmine replies. "He's on the building committee, and he says they are in a hurry to get it done."

"Next fall? I thought it would be ready in time for our musical," Holly says.

"Not a chance. They are going to work all through summer vacation," Princess comments.

We are interrupted by the loud *zing* of an electric saw.

When it finally stops, Holly asks, "Why can't the workers do this at night?"

"It's dark! Duh!" Carmelita replies.

"I suppose they could use really bright lights," Holly suggests.

"I think they're working day and night," Jasmine says.

"Mr. Wood really needs that music room," I tell them. "Is it true we're going to be able to have an orchestra?"

"Instruments are hard to learn. Singing is easy — all you have to do is open your mouth," Jasmine says.

"Easy for you to say," I reply with a giggle.

"We need to give Sassy a big horn!" Carmelita says.

I laugh with them. "If we do get to have an orchestra, and you could pick any instrument you wanted, which would you choose?"

Holly says, "The piano. Because that's the instrument we dance to in ballet class."

"Kinda hard to put it in your book bag!" I tell her. I bend over and pretend I'm walking with a piano on my back.

"I'd choose the harp," Princess says. "I think it sounds like angel music." That's a good choice. Princess has long, flowing blond hair. It ripples down her back like a golden stream. I think she looks like one of those angels on decorations during the Christmas season.

"All those strings," Carmelita says. "I bet your fingertips would get sore. Me, I'd pick something easy, like a drum. Just hit it with a stick and be done with it."

We crack up.

Jasmine then says, "I'd choose a trumpet because it's loud, and everyone would notice me."

She pretends to toot a horn. Then Carmelita beats on her pretend drum, while Princess strums her imaginary harp, and Holly moves her fingers over invisible piano keys. They've got quite a band going.

"What about you, Sassy? What instrument would *you* choose?" Jasmine asks me when they stop.

I pause a moment, then I say very quietly, "I'd choose the piccolo."

"What's a piccolo?" Princess asks. "It sounds like something good to eat."

"It's a tiny flute, and it plays pretty music way up high. It sounds like birds in the morning in springtime when you do it right."

"You sound like you know quite a bit about it," Holly says.

"I do." I finally decide to tell my friends what I've been up to. "I've been taking lessons since last year. Holly, just like you go to dance lessons, I go to a studio where I play the piccolo!"

"So this is the big secret?" Jasmine asks with her hands on her hips. "You could have told me, Sassy. I think it's really cool."

I give her a big smile of thanks. Then I tell everybody, "At first I was scared I wouldn't be any good at it — like my singing. So I never said anything to anybody."

"Not even your best friend?" Jasmine looks a little upset with me.

"I decided to wait and tell people if I ever got to be any good at it," I try to explain.

"So are you better at the piccolo than you are at singing?" Princess asks.

"*Much, much* better," I tell her.

"Prove it!" Jasmine says. Her voice says she's still not happy with me.

"Okay. I'll show you." I reach down into my Sassy Sack and pull out the black leather case.

"Ooh," they say with admiration in their voices.

"Only Sassy could find an instrument that's small enough to fit into that purse of hers," Carmelita says. The rest of the girls nod in agreement.

Slowly, I unlatch the case. Sitting in two parts is my shiny silver piccolo. It gleams in the sunlight. Tiny round silver keys line the surface. Each key, when pressed alone or with others, makes a different sound as I blow over the mouthpiece.

"It's silver!" Princess says.

"And beautiful!" Holly exclaims.

"Well, it's not made of *real* silver, but it's shiny enough for me to pretend," I say proudly.

I slip the two pieces together, place my fingers on the keys, purse my lips, and blow softly. A lovely, lilting melody comes out. I play a little song I learned a few months ago.

"Awesome!" Jasmine says. Her voice is warming up.

I keep on playing. Some of the other kids wander over to where we are.

Tandy, Travis, and Rusty look really surprised.

"What is that thing?" Travis asks. "It looks like a silver Popsicle!"

I ignore him and continue to play. I play trills and running notes. It sounds like rippling water.

I glance up and realize about twenty kids are around me, listening quietly and smiling. I finish the song, then stop. Then they clap and clap and clap. They cheer.

I can't believe it. They like my music!

I guess it's not a secret anymore.

CHAPTER SIX

Rehearsals Are Fun — Sort Of

Rehearsals are fun, but they are harder work than any of us thought. When school gets out, we have a snack and some juice, then head for the auditorium. Sometimes we practice the songs, and other times we go over the dances. Over and over and over. Mr. Wood says we have to practice many times so the show will be perfect.

Mr. Wood begins each rehearsal with all of us sitting on the stage in a circle. He says the same thing every day. "As you know, boys and girls, our show is called *Kids to the Rescue*. We want to demonstrate through music the importance of saving our planet, and the power kids have to make a difference. I believe in each and every one of you, and I'm proud we're working together on this project. Now, let's get busy!"

It's a good way to start. He makes us feel like we can do anything. We clap and cheer. Then I pull my clipboard out of my Sassy Sack and tell everyone what the schedule is for the day.

"Josephina, you and Jasmine go to the back row and practice your duet about the oceans."

"Gotcha."

Mr. Wood has rented several mini iPods and iPod players for our rehearsals, so each group can practice separately. For safekeeping, I keep the little iPods in my sack as well. I toss the blue one to Jasmine as she and Josephina head to the back.

I check them off with a blue marker — blue for the ocean song.

"Sassy!" Josephina says urgently as she turns around and hurries to me. "A button came off my blouse — right in front!" She holds her blouse together.

"Relax, Josie," I say. I reach down into my sack and pull out a miniature sewing kit that my mom brought home from a hotel stay. "I even have blue thread to match your shirt. Run to the restroom and whip on the button."

"I can't sew!" she replies desperately.

"I'm not so good at sewing myself," I tell her. "Here, take a couple of safety pins instead."

"That'll work. Thanks, Sassy!" She hurries to the bathroom to fix her blouse.

I check my clipboard. "Travis, you and Rusty and Charles

work on the dance for your trio. Make sure the music and the moves flow smoothly this time, okay?" I pull the small brown iPod out of my sack and give it to Travis.

"You got any Scotch tape in that bag of yours?" Travis asks. He holds a sheet of paper with the lyrics to their song. "We're gonna tape up the words on the wall so our hands are free to do our moves. We're tight!"

"Sure, Travis." I reach down into my sack and pull out a roll of tape.

The three boys give me a thumbs-up as they head out to the hallway, where they will practice a really funny song and dance called "Carbon Footprint." They get to stomp in army boots to the beat of lots of tom-toms. A perfect choice for them.

"I've got an idea," I tell them. "How about if you wear sunglasses while you do your number? It would send a message about the power of the sun. Plus, you'd look cool!"

"Great idea, Sassy," Travis says as I give them each a pair of shades from my sack. I send them off as I check their names on my list with a brown marker — brown for the earth.

Kevin, Abdul, and Ricky are performing a song about polar bears losing their habitat in the Arctic. It's called "Who Melted My Ice?"

"I'm going to order helium balloons for your song," I tell them. "I saw some at the party store last week. They're made of that shiny Mylar stuff, and they come shaped like squares!"

"Cool!" Abdul says. "Balloons that look like ice cubes!"

I give them a red iPod and check them off with my red marker — red meaning danger warnings for the bears.

"Holly, are you ready to practice your ballet solo?" I ask her.

She nods as she puts on her dance slippers. "I wish I could do the dance on pointe," she says wistfully, "but my teacher says I'm still too young for toe shoes."

I scrunch up my face. "I bet those shoes hurt your feet," I tell her. "Your dance is really pretty, and you can move easier in your slippers, right?"

"You're right, Sassy," she says. "I'm glad Mr. Wood made you stage manager. You know just what to say!"

I'm amazed. I've never been in charge of anything, but this seems easy to me. I like telling other people what to do for a change!

Holly uses the big music player on the stage as she practices. I check her off on my sheet — green for the dance about the rain forest.

Mr. Wood runs from group to group, making suggestions,

making improvements, and giving words of encouragement. "Lovely!" he calls out to Holly, who moves like a leaf in the wind.

"That's going to look awesome when we do it in costume," he says to Jasmine and Josephina. "Super!"

I try not to care how they will look in those shimmery dresses. I give them both a smile of encouragement anyway.

After twenty minutes or so, Mr. Wood calls the entire choir to the stage to practice the group songs. They will be wearing the awesome purple costumes for the performance.

I sit in the front row with my clipboard and strawberry-scented marker. I check all the kids off my list. I keep telling myself that it doesn't matter that I'm not up there with them.

Mr. Wood announces, "Tomorrow's rehearsal will be a little different, folks. We're going to try it with some of the props and costumes."

Jasmine looks really excited. So do Holly and Carmelita.

"Sassy, I'll really need your help tomorrow. I know you have a list of what everyone needs for each number, so I'll be depending on you to make everything run smoothly."

"Sure thing," I tell him with a smile. But inside I'm not so happy.

"So," Mr. Wood says as he takes a deep breath, "let's make today's run-through really great!"

Everybody seems to be excited as they take their places.

One of the songs the entire choir sings is called "Let's Go Green." It's all about recycling and global warming and stuff. Mr. Wood wrote the song himself and it's really good. It's a funny song, but it gets the point across.

Mr. Wood told us he has an organic garden in his yard, he never uses plastic bottles, and he heats his house with solar panels. I admire that.

There's also a trio made up of Basima, Iris, and Misty. They are singing a song called "Pull the Plug." Their voices blend just perfectly. Iris is a soprano, Basima is an alto, and Misty's voice fits right in the middle. Their props are extension cords — purple ones. I wonder where Mr. Wood found them.

"I have an idea," I tell the three girls. I reach down into my sack and pull out a dozen lavender-and-violet-colored metallic bangle bracelets. "Try these. The bracelets will rattle on your arms and make a nice sound as you sing."

"You've got everything in that sack, Sassy," Iris says, awestruck.

"I like to be prepared," I say simply. I check them off with a purple marker.

The next song sung by the entire choir is just plain hot. It's called "Purple Passion for Icy Blue Waters." It's all about saving the earth and making a difference. It sounds a little like a rock version of "America the Beautiful," and it makes me want to save the planet right away. I guess that's the point.

Even though it's a group song, Travis and Princess each get a solo. Travis sings a verse about the land, and Princess sings a really pretty melody about the sea. The whole choir sings the chorus, and even the audience can join in.

For the very last number, the entire choir is also singing a popular song called "What a Wonderful World." A video will show images of green fields and rainbows and lovely sunsets. While the choir hums, Carmelita sings her solo. It's so pretty that people in the audience will need a tissue to wipe their eyes.

It will be a bang-up finale.

Just as Mr. Wood raises his baton to start the "Purple Passion" song, he notices Princess is not onstage.

"She had to go to the bathroom," I tell him.

"Again?" he asks.

I think she runs in there every fifteen minutes.

Holly told me that Princess likes to comb her hair and make sure it's just right, so when she hurries back onto the risers, I say, "Your hair looks really nice, Princess." She smiles and sings her solo perfectly.

Gee, I'm good at this.

CHAPTER SEVEN

Fire!

Mr. Wood comes to school the next day wearing a navy blue T-shirt with a giant picture of the earth on the front. The words SAVE ME are printed in a bold red under the photo of the planet.

"I guess he means save the earth, not save *him*," Travis whispers as Mr. Wood bounds into the music room.

Rusty laughs so hard he almost falls out of his chair.

"It's so not fair that teachers get to wear whatever they want, but we have to wear these boring blue-and-white uniforms!" I whisper back.

"Tell me about it!" Holly adds.

"It *is* a nice shirt," Jasmine says.

"Let's get our voices warmed up," Mr. Wood says after he marks attendance. "Take your places on the risers, please."

I don't even bother to go up and pretend to sing anymore. I get my clipboard out of my Sassy Sack, get the iPods from the storage room, toss those into my bag, and go over my list for rehearsal after school.

The voices of the choir begin to sing loud and clear, *"From the golden valleys of the earth to the purple sunsets on the beach, we sing of Mother Earth and all her glory. . . ."*

But even *louder* noises interrupt us.

SCREEEE! SCREEEE!

THUMPA-THUMPA-THUMPA-BAM!

"What was that?" Travis yells.

Mr. Wood gives the class the signal to stop singing. "The construction people," he replies with a sigh. "How are we to conduct rehearsal with all that racket?"

SCREEEE! SCREEEE!

THUMPA-THUMPA-THUMPA-BAM!

"Not very well," Travis says, speaking for all of us.

Silence returns for a moment. Mr. Wood lifts his arms to signal the choir to begin.

"From the golden valleys of the earth to the purple sunsets on the beach, we sing of Mother Earth and all her glory. . . ."

THUMPA-THUMPA-THUMPA-BAM!

SCREEEE! SCREEEE!

"I'm getting a headache!" I complain.

Holly sits in the first row of seats next to me, waiting until she is called up for her dance solo.

"Do you have some hand sanitizer?" she whispers.

"Everything is so dirty around here with all this building and stuff. I like to stay fresh."

I give her an understanding smile, pull out a peppermint-scented sanitizer spray from my sack, and hand it to her. "You're right," I say. "Dirt is everywhere!"

I glance outside. Even the classroom windows are glazed with grime. This place is a mess. I squirt a little sanitizer on my own hands before I toss it back into my sack.

"Let's try it again, my young singers," Mr. Wood says. He raises his baton, and the group starts to sing once more.

"From the golden valleys of the earth to the purple sunsets on the beach, we sing of Mother Earth and all her glory. . . ."

THUMPA-THUMPA-THUMPA-BAM!

THUMPA-THUMPA-THUMPA-BAM!

THUMPA-THUMPA-THUMPA-BAM!

If he wasn't bald, I think Mr. Wood might have ripped out his hair. He stomps toward the classroom door. His face is red with anger.

Travis and Rusty, standing on the first row of risers, crack up. "I want Mr. Wood on my team," Travis yells out.

"Yeah, he's tough when it comes to looking out for us," Rusty agrees.

Before Mr. Wood reaches the door, it is flung open and one of the construction workers strides in. He's a big man — much taller than Mr. Wood and way more muscular. He's wearing a T-shirt with the sleeves cut off, so his thick arms make him look really powerful. He is so tall that Mr. Wood has to look up at him.

"They look like two cowboys ready to have a shoot-out," Holly says.

"Yeah, but only the worker guy has a weapon!" I reply. "Look at that cool utility belt around his waist."

Filled with hammers and screwdrivers and wrenches, his leather belt hangs low around his jeans. He wears thick brown boots covered with dirt.

Mr. Wood demands loudly, "Are you aware this is a school? We are trying to conduct classes!"

The man replies with a deep, powerful bass voice, "I'm sorry, sir, but the board of education is rushing us to get this job finished. I know it's a pain."

"Can't you just wait until school gets out before you start the loud banging and thumping? We're trying to sing in here!"

"Several other teachers have complained as well," the worker explains. "I just came in to tell you we should be done with this side of the building in three days."

"Well, that's good news," Mr. Wood says, calming down a little.

"My name is Bike," the worker explains, offering his huge, glove-covered hand to Mr. Wood.

"I'm Randall Wood, the music teacher," Mr. Wood says as he shakes Bike's hand.

"Yeah, I could hear the choir even out in the hall. The kids are really good. I wish I could sing like that."

"You'll have to come to our show," Mr. Wood says proudly.

"I might just do that," Bike says as he turns to leave. "I like your shirt, man," he tells Mr. Wood. "I'm all for saving the planet."

Mr. Wood looks both pleased and relieved. After Bike leaves, we manage to get through all of the songs without any more interruptions.

When the bell signals the end of class, Mr. Wood announces, "Grab a snack and let's head for the auditorium. We'll start rehearsal in fifteen minutes."

I grab my Sassy Sack and my clipboard and take a juice box from my sack. As I sip, I check my list.

Shades for Travis, Rusty, and Charles. Check.

Sparkly vests for all the boys. Check.

The girls are not going to wear their dresses yet. Good.

Video player for the "Wonderful World" song. Already in the auditorium. Check.

Green Easter basket grass for Holly's rain forest dance. Check.

I'll need lots more stuff for future rehearsals, but this is plenty for now. I grab as much as I can carry and plop it down in the front of the auditorium. Then I go back and get the rest.

"Are we ready, Sassy?" Mr. Wood asks. I can't believe a teacher is asking me if we can start!

"Yes, we are," I reply.

"Boys, go and get your vests from Sassy," Mr. Wood says.

They tromp over to me and I hand them each a shiny vest.

"How come the boys get to wear their vests and we can't practice in our dresses?" Jasmine asks.

"Because they can slip the vests over their shirts," Mr. Wood replies. "Don't worry — we will have a full dress rehearsal before the show, and you can all make sure the dresses fit perfectly."

Jasmine seems satisfied with this, and I hand her the blue hula hoops, which are supposed to show the movement of the oceans and the tides.

We can hear the workers in the distance, but the auditorium walls are pretty thick. So the screeching and thumping are not so bad.

Everyone has their props, and we are ready to begin.

"Let's see if we can get through the first song without interruptions," Mr. Wood exclaims.

The choir sounds great. Travis is remembering the words. Princess has not run out to the bathroom. Rusty almost falls off a riser, but everyone keeps on singing. Even I'm impressed with how good they sound.

Holly does her dance perfectly. I make a note on my clipboard to tell the lighting guy to make the background green for her piece.

Travis and Rusty and Charles put the mike down near their boots so the stomping is even louder. Everybody cracks up as they dance and sing. It's hard for everyone to sing the words right because they keep laughing at the three boys. That's going to be one of the best parts of the show.

When we get to "What a Wonderful World," I walk to the middle row and click on the video player. I make a note on my clipboard, *Have Tony, the guy running the lights, play the video.* I can't do everything.

The background changes colors with the pictures of all the beautiful parts of the world. The kids sing about trees and roses. As I stand by the video player, I'm carried away by how great they sound and how well the pictures match the words.

It's almost time for Carmelita's solo. I point to her to give her the cue, but she's ready. She takes a deep breath and starts singing about skies and clouds.

Suddenly, *Wee-waw, wee-waw, wee-waw!* The piercing sound of the fire alarm breaks the lovely mood. Carmelita stops singing and looks around in confusion.

"What's going on?" she asks.

"A fire drill *after* school?" Travis yells. "Now I've seen everything!"

But Mr. Wood does not take time to act confused. He leaps into action. "Off the stage!" he cries. "Hurry!"

Some kids jump off the stage. Others hurry down the steps. Everybody heads for the back doors.

Then Bike rushes into the auditorium. "This is not a drill!" he shouts loudly in his deep bass voice. "It's a real fire! Get out! Get out! Get out now!"

My heart starts to beat really fast. *Fire?*

Mr. Wood asks no questions but continues to rush everyone out of the room. "Quickly, children!" he cries. "Leave everything!"

Kids are hurrying down the aisle. I can smell smoke.

Jasmine grabs my hand. "Come on, Sassy! We have to get out of here!" Bike takes her other hand and rushes us outside. Then he runs back in.

Boys in sparkly vests are hurrying out the back door of the auditorium. Holly wears her dance shoes. Carmelita looks scared. But all of us get outside in no time. Mr. Wood and Bike are the last ones to come out of the building.

"Is everyone here?" Bike asks.

Mr. Wood counts heads and then counts us again. "Yes. Thankfully. All my students are here and safe."

We can hear the fire sirens. They sound really close. Then a bright green fire truck turns the corner.

"Awesome!" Travis makes fire siren noises of his own.

Jasmine and I roll our eyes.

"I thought all fire trucks were red," Holly says.

"Some are bright green," Rusty explains, "so that cars can see them better."

This time Rusty and Abdul roll their eyes at us.

"What happened?" Mr. Wood asks Bike as the firemen rush inside.

"One of us was working with a torch and a little spark flew in the wrong direction," Bike explains.

"What burned?" Travis asks.

"Just a pile of trash and sawdust our cleanup crew had left in the lobby of the auditorium," Bike replies. "It's not a big fire — we actually just about put it out ourselves."

"So why the fire department?" Abdul wonders.

"Oh, we're required by law to make sure our workplace is safe for the workers as well as for the students. The fire department has to make an investigation and file a report, and will probably give us a citation for being unsafe." He looks unhappy about that.

"Will we be able to continue rehearsal now?" Mr. Wood asks him.

"Oh, no, sir. You can send the kids home. The auditorium will be off-limits for several hours."

"For a trash fire?"

"Sorry." Bike shrugs. "Rules. Regulations. Legalities. You understand."

Mr. Wood turns to me. "Sassy, please collect all the vests and the props. I'll put them in my car. Then I'll take everyone to the office so you can call your parents to pick you up early. They will be worried when they hear news of a fire at school."

I nod at him, look at my clipboard, and reach down into my sack for a marker.

My heart starts to beat faster than when they yelled "Fire!" My sack is not on my shoulder! Then I remember. I went to turn on the video player. I left my bag in the front row of the auditorium. Then Jasmine grabbed my hand and we ran out with Bike.

I gasp as I realize what has happened. My Sassy Sack is still in there with all my stuff! OMG, my piccolo!

CHAPTER EIGHT

The Sassy Sack Is Missing!

"Mr. Wood!" I cry out in alarm. "I have to go back in the auditorium! My Sassy Sack is in there!"

"Your what?"

"My Sassy Sack. My purse. My bag." My stomach feels gurgly. "I have to get it out of the auditorium. Please."

"I'm sorry, Sassy, but you're not going to be able to get back in there this afternoon. It will be fine, and you can get it first thing in the morning."

"But I *never* go *anywhere* without it!" I wail.

"It's just a purse."

"No, it's not! It's part of *me*. It's got all my important stuff in there!"

"I'm sure whatever is in there will be just fine until tomorrow."

"Please!" I beg.

"I can't, Sassy. The fire department has blocked all the doors. Nobody can get back in there. Not you. Not me."

I sit down on the grass and hold my head my hands. I gulp loudly. I'm trying not to cry.

Jasmine sits down next to me and puts her arm around my shoulders. "It will be okay, Sassy. Your sack will be waiting for you in the morning."

"But it's never been away from me — not since I got it when I was seven years old. Never." I feel cold and I shiver.

"I know," she says, giving me a big hug. "This is just plain terrible!"

I try once more to convince Mr. Wood. "If I don't come home with that bag, I'll be in big trouble with my mom."

"I'm sure she'll understand that it was an emergency situation," Mr. Wood says in that voice that grown-ups use to quiet kids who are upset.

I'm feeling desperate. "But I have something *really* special in there," I tell him. "It's kind of expensive. My mother will not be happy if I don't come home with it."

"You know you're not supposed to bring expensive items to school, Sassy," Mr. Wood says in a warning voice. "Is it a video game player?"

"No," I say quietly.

"A cell phone?"

"My mother won't let me have one," I tell him.

"Then what is it?" he asks gently. He sounds like he really does feel sorry for me.

I take a deep breath. "It's my instrument — my piccolo."

"You play the piccolo?"

"Yes. For the past year or so."

"And she's really good at it," Jasmine adds. "She plays *way* better than she sings!"

I smile a tiny little smile.

Mr. Wood grins. "Well, that's wonderful news, Sassy! I can't wait until the construction is completed and we have our new orchestra room. I'd love to hear you play."

"I can't play it if it's missing," I tell him quietly.

"It's not missing. It's in your bag, which is in the auditorium, which is locked down until morning."

"I just gotta have that bag!" I say helplessly. "It's like my third hand."

"Yeah, the hand with all the rings and ribbons and ruffles," Holly says, joining us. "Sassy really does need that bag, Mr. Wood. She's just not Sassy without it."

Mr. Wood looks like he almost understands how bad I feel. Almost. "I wish I could do something, but I can't," he tells me.

"Bike, can you help me?" I turn to him, pleading.

"Sorry, kid," Bike says, shaking his head. "Fire marshal says nobody gets in there. Nobody. I'm really sorry."

Mr. Wood reaches out a hand to help me stand up. I rise slowly. "What am I going to do?" I ask Jasmine. I feel so empty and lost without my Sassy Sack.

"Let's go call your mom, explain to her what happened, and then we can all go out for pizza to help make you feel better."

"I don't think I can eat," I whisper. "I just want to go home and pray for it to be morning."

She squeezes my hand. I'm glad she's my friend. She understands how bad I feel.

Mr. Wood gathers up the vests and props that kids have left on the grass next to me. I glance back at the firemen swarming all over. Then we all walk slowly to the school office.

I wait in line with the other kids who don't have cell phones and I call Mom. "Can you pick me up early?" I ask.

"Sure, Sassy. Rehearsal is over already?"

"There was a fire at school."

"Fire? Oh, my goodness!"

"It was just a little trash fire in the lobby of the auditorium. It was no big deal."

"A fire at school is *always* a big deal! Are you okay?"

"I'm fine, Mom. There was just a little smoke by the time the firefighters got here."

"Firefighters? I'm rushing right over there!"

"Mom, listen. I'm fine. The fire was tiny, but because it was caused by the workers who are doing the school construction, they have to file safety reports and stuff. So they locked down the auditorium."

"Well, that's a good thing. I'm glad they are worrying about safety."

"No, Mom, that's *not* a good thing. They locked my Sassy Sack in the auditorium and they won't let me go back in there! Mom, what am I gonna do?"

"I'll be right over, Sassy. We'll figure something out."

I hang up the phone and let the next kid call home.

I tell Jasmine, "My mom is on her way. You want a ride home?"

"Thanks, but my mother will be here in a minute. She heard about the fire on the news and she jumped in her car to come and get me. She said the report made it seem like it was a huge, flaming firestorm."

"I'm glad it wasn't," I tell her. "But I wish they'd let me get my bag."

"Yeah, I know." Jasmine touches me on the arm.

When Mom arrives, she hugs me, then says, "Are you all right, Sassy?" She looks concerned — I guess because of all the fire equipment still sitting in front of the school.

"I'm fine, Mom. The school is fine. It was just a small fire. But my Sassy Sack is . . ." I can't even finish the sentence.

Mom gives me a bear hug this time. "It will be morning before you know it," she says. "Let's go home and get some dinner, okay?"

"But my piccolo is in my sack, Mom. What about my lesson?" In all the time I've been taking lessons, I've only missed one, and that was because Mrs. Rossini was sick.

"We'll call Mrs. Rossini, explain to her what happened, and I'm sure we can reschedule your lesson."

"Mom, can't *you* make them open the auditorium so I can get my sack?"

She kneels down in front of me so she can look me in the eye. "No, Sassy, I can't. But I'll come with you in the morning to make sure we get in there first thing, okay?"

I nod, but nothing is really okay.

Jasmine's mom rushes in with lots of other scared parents. Mr. Wood explains to everyone what happened, and that there is nothing to worry about.

But I've got big worries.

Jasmine and I wave good-bye, and we both get in our cars so our moms can drive us home.

When we get to our house I ask Mom, "Can I call Grammy?"

"I think that's a great idea, Sassy." She hands me the phone, and I punch in the numbers.

Grammy's voice always makes me feel better. "Hi, Sassy," she says cheerfully. "I'm so glad you called! How was your day?"

"Not good, Grammy."

Instantly, her voice sounds soothing, like a hug. "What's wrong?"

"My Sassy Sack is missing!" I whisper into the phone.

"Oh, Sassy! I know you must be hurting. What happened?"

I tell her about the workers and the fire and the locked auditorium. "I've never been without it, Grammy. Not since you gave it to me."

"I'm sure it will be waiting for you in the morning. It's probably missing you, too."

She makes me giggle a little.

"How are rehearsals going for the show?" Grammy asks. I think she's trying to change the subject.

"Pretty good," I tell her.

"Poppy and I are going to come and see it, you know."

"But I'm not in it!" I remind her.

"You're the stage manager, aren't you?"

"Yes, but I have to be backstage the whole time."

"Would the show be successful without you?"

"I don't know. I guess not. I like being in charge."

"I know you do. You're a natural leader, Miss Sassy!"

She makes me feel proud.

"But you don't have to come all the way from Florida just to see a show where I'll be behind the curtain the whole time."

I tell her this, but I hope she comes anyway. I love being with Grammy.

"Didn't I come when Sadora had one line in her school play?"

"Yep. All she had to do was announce, 'Welcome to the Alcazar!' to the actors onstage."

"And didn't I come when Sabin's picture was chosen for the art show?"

"Of course he painted a plate of food!" I say with a laugh.

"So you know I'll be there to see the show that you're stage managing."

"Thanks, Grammy," I tell her. "I can't wait to see you."

"I'll see you soon, Sassy. I know you'll find your sack tomorrow."

I feel better when I hang up. But I still worry about my Sassy Sack. It's all alone in that big old auditorium. Without me.

So is my piccolo.

CHAPTER NINE

Lost, and Finally Found

The next morning I am awake, up, and dressed before anybody in the house. I'm actually surprised that I was able to sleep at all.

I'm dressed in my dumb old blue-and-white school uniform, waiting at the kitchen table, when Mom comes downstairs to fix breakfast.

"Oh, my!" she says. "You surprised me."

"Can we go early, Mom? Please?"

"You need to eat breakfast first, Sassy. But I promise I'll get you there as quickly as I can."

She pours me a glass of orange juice, but I just sip it.

"Your hair is a mess," Mom says. "Hand me your brush so I can tame it a little."

"My brush is in my Sassy Sack," I reply glumly.

"Oh, yes. I forgot. Sorry, Sassy." She starts to scramble

some eggs. I feel like those eggs this morning — all scrambled and runny and broken.

Sadora comes into the kitchen next. She goes to high school and gets to wear whatever she wants to school. Today she's wearing a short gold skirt, yellow leggings, and an orange sweater. She looks like sunlight to me.

"Hey, Little Sister," she says as she pours juice for herself. "I'm so sorry about your sack. But you'll get it back this morning, and that Sassy smile will come back to your face."

I try to smile for her. As older sisters go, she's pretty cool. She just got her driver's license, and sometimes Mom will let her drive me and my friends to the mall. Sometimes she even gives me extra spending money when we get there.

Then Sabin and Zero bound into the kitchen. "Hey, Sassy! Can I get a candy bar? How about a Band-Aid for my pinkie finger? You got a couple of pencils I can hold till school gets out? And maybe some paper clips for my project?" Then my brother laughs and tries to tickle me.

I just glare, then throw my toast at him. He knows all that stuff is in my bag. He ducks, and Zero makes a perfect catch, gobbling the toast in one swallow.

"Don't worry, Little Sister. You'll be cool soon when you've got that thing slung across your chest once more. I don't know how you even keep up with all that junk in there!"

"Sabin, don't tease your sister," Mom says. "Suppose you lost something very special to you."

"It's not lost!" I tell Mom. "It's just locked up in the auditorium." I get up from the table. "I'm waiting in the car."

Sabin actually forgets most of his stuff every day. He *finally* gets in the car after he has to run back into the house for his sneakers, his lunch, and his violin. I don't say anything. I just want them to hurry up.

When we finally get to my school, Mom goes with me to the office.

"We're trying to find a lost item that was left in the auditorium yesterday," Mom explains to the secretary. "My daughter's purse."

It is *so* much more than a purse to me, but I don't say anything.

"Not a problem, ma'am," she replies. "Everything is unlocked now and ready for the school day. Feel free to go and get what you need."

We head down the hall and around the corner toward the auditorium. The bell has not yet rung for class. Lots of kids are in the hall, talking or reading or playing video games. Travis rolls by in those tennis shoes with built-in wheels. He waves as he passes us.

I feel funny walking with my mother. I wonder if kids think I'm in trouble.

When we get to the lobby of the auditorium, I can see a small black area on the floor where the fire had been. Everything else has been swept clean.

Mom pulls open the door. The auditorium lights are on, and it looks exactly as we'd left it. The video player is still in the middle row, Rusty's science book is on the floor where he'd dropped it, and two hula hoops lay on the stage. I run full speed down the aisle to the front row. I could have beaten Travis on his shoe skates.

I'm smiling before I even get to the front of the auditorium. I reach the front row and extend my hands to grab that bag. But it's not there. *It's not there!*

I look under the seats. Nothing. I check the next row. Nothing. My heart is starting to beat really fast.

Mom approaches me and asks, "Where is it, Sassy?"

I'm almost afraid to answer. "I don't know, Mom. It's not where I left it!"

I check under every single seat in every single row in the auditorium. My hands and the knees of my slacks get filthy. Mom helps. She checks the stage area, backstage, even the dressing room and the room where they keep costumes for the drama class.

But my Sassy Sack is not to be found. It's gone.

"Mom!" I gasp. "What am I going to do?" I'm trying not to cry, but I am very close.

Mom puts her arm around my shoulders. "Let's go back to the office," she says gently. "We'll let them know it's missing."

Missing! My sack is missing. Gone. Hiding. Lost. Maybe stolen. I think I might throw up.

When we get back to the office, the secretary, Mrs. Starr, looks up from her computer. "Did you find what you were looking for?" she asks with a pleasant smile.

"No, we didn't," Mom replies. "My daughter's purse was left in the auditorium yesterday in all the confusion of the fire. But it is not there now. We searched everywhere. It's just not there."

Mrs. Starr looks a little concerned but she says, "I'm sure it will turn up. Describe it for me so I can be on the lookout if it gets turned in to our lost-and-found box."

I think about the dirty gym shoes and torn hoodies and unwashed T-shirts that collect in that lost-and-found box. I can't bear the thought of my sack being tossed in there.

"What's your name, sweetie?" Mrs. Starr asks. She picks up a yellow pencil.

"Sassy," I manage to say. "Sassy Simone Sanford."

"And what grade are you in?"

"Fourth."

Mrs. Starr continues to write. "And you say you lost your purse? Can you describe it?"

Of course I can describe it! Grown-ups ask the silliest questions.

"It's purple," I say in a small voice. "And pink, magenta, and silver. It's made of lots of different fabrics. And it's got sparkles on it — sequins and gems."

I touch the place on my hip where my sack should be. I almost feel naked without it.

Mrs. Starr looks up. "I've seen you in the halls with that bag, dear. I've always admired it. I thought you'd lost an ordinary purse."

"My grandmother made it for me. There is no other purse like it in the whole world." I gulp.

Mom puts her arm around my shoulders again. "We'll find it, Sassy," she assures me.

"Can you tell me what was in it?" Mrs. Starr asks.

"A million things," I tell her. "Gum, pens, nail polish, lotion, lip gloss, jewelry, glue, batteries, mirror, tape." I pause. "Everything I need is in there."

"And everything anyone else needs as well," Mom adds. "Sassy's sack seems to hold the perfect solution for whatever is needed. It's a treasure trove."

"Was there any money in the bag?" Mrs. Starr asks.

"I think I had two quarters and a nickel in my change purse. I care more about the purse. It has my name on it."

Mrs. Starr smiles. "Was there anything of value in the bag, Sassy?"

"Well, I'm the stage manager for the spring concert, and I had several mini iPods in there. Mr. Wood takes them out of the cabinet and gives them to me. I give them to the performers and we put everything back after practice. But we had to leave early. So the music players are still in my bag."

"Hmm," says Mrs. Starr as she scribbles. "Is there anything else in the bag that you want me to be aware of?"

"Yes," I say slowly. "My instrument is in my bag. I've already missed one lesson. I don't want to miss another."

I feel sniffly and I need a tissue, but, of course, my tissues are in my sack.

"What musical instrument is small enough to fit into a purse?" asks Mrs. Starr.

"I play the piccolo. It's little, just like me."

Mom says, "What else can be done to help locate the bag, Mrs. Starr?"

"I'll ask all the custodians if they've seen it, and I'll send an e-mail to everyone on staff," she tells Mom. "Your bag will turn up, Sassy," Mrs. Starr says in a kind voice. "As soon as it does, I'll call you down to the office, okay?"

"Okay." But I'm still feeling pretty scared. Where could it be?

Mrs. Starr gives me a pass to get to class, and Mom hugs me once more before she leaves.

The day drags on. I can't laugh at Travis even though he bumps into a wall with those wheeled shoes. I can't concentrate on my math. And I sure can't eat lunch.

When it's time for choir, I walk in slowly and sadly.

Mr. Wood says, "I got the e-mail Mrs. Starr sent this morning, Sassy. I went back and searched the auditorium again. I'm so sorry, but I could not find your bag."

My shoulders slump.

"What about the iPods?" I ask him.

"We'll do without them today. I have all the music saved on a zip drive, so we'll be okay until your bag shows up."

"You think it will?"

"I sure hope so," he says.

He continues, and I go over my notes on my clipboard. But my heart is not in it. I listen to the songs, but they sound gray to me today instead of bright and colorful.

No construction sounds interrupt us today.

It's almost time for the bell. Mr. Wood is giving directions. The door opens, and Bike walks in.

"Hello, Bike," Mr. Wood says. "Thanks for the peace and quiet today."

Bike grins. "After all the problems caused by the fire

yesterday, my boss said we work in student areas only after every child has left the building."

"Great idea. That probably should have been the rule from the beginning," Mr. Wood says.

Bike turns to leave, then says, "Oh, I almost forgot!" He removes a leather backpack he'd been wearing. "Did anybody leave this in the auditorium yesterday?" He looks directly at me and grins. "I found it after everyone left, and I locked it up for safekeeping."

From the backpack he pulls my beautiful, incredible bag. I squeal with excitement and run over to him.

"My sack! You found my Sassy Sack!"

"Sure is a pretty thing," Bike says as he hands it to me. "I bet my daughter would love to have one just like it."

As I take it from him, I touch it gently. I breathe deeply as I sling it over my shoulder and across my chest. I peek inside. Everything is still there. Including my piccolo. And the iPods.

"Thank you. Thank you. Thank you," I whisper. "Thank you so much."

CHAPTER TEN

Piccolo Lesson

Saturday morning, instead of sleeping in, I head to my makeup piccolo lesson. Mrs. Rossini looks alert and ready, not sleepy like me.

I take the piccolo out of my sack, but I leave the bag on. After yesterday, I'm not going to separate myself from it anymore. I even slept with my Sassy Sack last night!

I carefully remove the piccolo from its case. I'm still amazed at how lovely it is. I slip the two pieces together and shine it a little with the soft cloth I keep tucked in my sack.

"I understand your piccolo went missing for a day or so," Mrs. Rossini says.

"I was really scared," I admit. "My purse got locked in a storage cabinet by the construction workers at our school."

"I'm glad you found it," Mrs. Rossini says. "Have you had time to practice?"

"Yes, I did," I tell her. "I really like the new song you gave me."

"Let's begin with our warm-ups then, shall we?" Mrs. Rossini says.

I place the piccolo very close to my bottom lip.

"Relax your facial muscles, Sassy. Let's aim for an easy, light *embouchure*."

I take the instrument away from my lips for a moment. "That sure is a funny word," I tell her. "Every time you say it, I want to giggle a little."

"Me, too," she admits. "The word is French. *Bouche* means 'mouth,' so *embouchure* simply refers to how you shape your lips to the mouthpiece."

"I know," I tell her. "My friend Holly takes ballet and she knows lots of French words from dance class."

"Are you stalling, Sassy?" Mrs. Rossini asks as she tilts her head to one side.

"A little," I admit. I smile and place the instrument to my lips once more.

"Let's begin with long tones," she says.

I blow softly and easily.

"Let the air do most of the work. Blow *across* the mouthpiece."

I do as she tells me.

"Now short, quick notes," she instructs.

This is so much fun! I love the squeakiness of the instrument, the lightness of the tones.

"Can you make it sound like a chirping bird?"

"I think so," I reply. I pause for a moment, place my fingers on the tiny silver keys, and trill.

"Very good!" Mrs. Rossini says, clapping her hands. "Now let's hear your piece for this week."

I place the sheet music on the stand in front of me and play a song called "Trees in the Valley." The music really does sound like wind blowing through leaves.

"You know, Sassy," Mrs. Rossini says when I stop to take a sip of water. "You certainly do show true talent for the piccolo. It's not an easy instrument to learn."

"Thank you," I reply.

"Let me try something else," she says. She goes to the piano and plays a simple tune — "Mary Had a Little Lamb."

"Can you play this?"

"Sure." I play the song without a hitch.

"What about this?" She plays a much harder piano piece.

I listen, think, then play it back for her on the piccolo.

"Amazing!" she says. "Very few children as young as you have the ability to listen to a song and then play it by ear. You are truly gifted."

Gifted? Me? The thought makes me smile broadly.

Mrs. Rossini starts to say something else, but she starts coughing. "Excuse me," she says. She sips some water but continues to cough.

I reach down into my sack and pull out a cough drop. "Will this help?" I ask her.

"Thank you, dear." She takes it, and her coughing eases up.

We continue the lesson. I like the way she pushes me to catch the right note and create the perfect sound.

Near the end of the hour she says, "Here is your assignment for next week. I'm looking forward to hearing you play this new piece."

As I tuck everything back into my sack, I discover the bundle of tickets for our show. Each student is supposed to sell five tickets. That's easy for me, because with my parents and brother and sister, as well as Grammy and Poppy, I'm already at six. But then I have an idea.

"Would you like to come to our school choir show?" I ask. "The tickets are only five dollars."

"When is it?"

"Next Thursday."

"Are you singing?"

"No. I can't sing. Not even a little bit."

"But you have so much musical ability!"

"Not in my vocal cords!"

We both laugh.

"I'm stage manager. But it's going to be a really good show, and all the proceeds will go to help us with Earth Day projects."

"I'll take a ticket, and if my schedule allows, I'll try to see the show. Is Mr. Wood still the music teacher there?" she asks as she notices the name of my school. "He and I went to college together."

"Yes, he's the choir director, and he hopes to start an orchestra in our school when the construction is finished and we have a room for it."

"What does he think of your ability on the piccolo?" Mrs. Rossini asks.

"Oh, he's never heard me play," I explain.

"Why not?"

"Well, since we don't have an orchestra yet there's really no point," I tell her.

"Will you play for him when he gets his orchestra room?"

"Should I?" I ask with a grin.

"Absolutely!" she says. She gives me a high five.

"Can I ask you something?" I say quietly.

"Of course, dear."

"Do you know that song 'What a Wonderful World'?"

"Oh, yes. It's one of my favorites," Mrs. Rossini replies with a smile.

"Can you play a little of it?" I ask her. I take my piccolo out of my sack and snap it back together.

She plays the song that Carmelita and the others will sing in the show.

"I want to see if I can play it on my piccolo," I tell her. "It's such a pretty song."

Mrs. Rossini smiles and plays the first few notes on her piano. I play them right after her on my piccolo. She plays more of the song. I follow her with the exact tune. Even though I don't have the sheet music, I play it just by listening. We finish the song — piano and piccolo — at the same time. It was just so lovely.

"Wow, Sassy. You rock." She looks really impressed. I feel so proud.

I grin at her as I put my instrument away once more.

"I can't wait until next year when we get our orchestra at school," I tell her.

"Mr. Wood will be glad to have you part of it," she tells me with confidence.

"I hope you can come to our show," I tell her as I head out the door.

"I'll try. Have a great day, Sassy."

I think I just might do that! I wave to Mrs. Rossini, then I look up at the sunshine as I head to Mom's car in the parking lot.

CHAPTER ELEVEN

Secrets of the Sassy Sack

I should be feeling really good. My Sassy Sack has been found. Mrs. Rossini says I'm pretty good on the piccolo. I'm going to the mall with Jasmine after dress rehearsal this afternoon. Grammy and Poppy will arrive here tomorrow morning. The show is tomorrow night, and it's going to rock.

Practice is going very smoothly. It really makes a difference with the workers not bumping and thumping around us.

I hate that I'll be backstage the whole time. Bummer.

But I'm really good at this stage manager job. I know the words and tune to every single song. I know all the light cues. We've got green for Holly's rain forest dance and blue for Josephina and Jasmine's duet.

Kids come to me with questions, and I actually know the answers!

"Hey, Sassy, where is the portable mike?"

"In the silver box on the left-hand side of the stage."

"Sassy, my mom wants to know how many feet of shiny blue cloth we'll need to make the fake ocean," Misty says.

I take a calculator out of my Sassy Sack and punch a couple of buttons. "We'll need six feet of cloth. Tell your mom we'll need it first thing in the morning. And tell her thanks."

"Sassy, who gets to shake the two ends of the cloth? That's a cool job," Iris wants to know.

"Why don't you and Misty do that," I suggest. "Your song is not until later in the show."

"Oh, thanks, Sassy!" they say. "You're the best!"

I can't believe people think I'm cool.

"Sassy, I can't find my sunglasses!" Travis cries out, alarm in his voice.

"You left them on the stage yesterday," I tell him. I pull them out of my sack and toss them to him.

"Thanks!"

"Sassy, I gotta go to the bathroom!" Princess says just as we're getting ready to start. She has her brush in her hand.

I pull a mirror out of my sack and hand it to her. "Use this instead," I whisper. She smiles and hurries onto the stage.

Carmelita is sneezing. "I don't feel good, Sassy," she says. "I think I'm getting a cold."

"You're not allowed to get sick!" I tell her. "Not until the show is over."

I give her a handful of the cough drops I offered to Mrs. Rossini, and a full package of pink tissues.

She keeps sneezing.

Mr. Wood calls us all to the stage before we begin the final run-through.

"This is it, children," he begins. "Dress rehearsal. We're going to run it like the real show. Costumes, lights, props — no stopping and starting. It's going to be a wonderful show and I'm very proud of every single one of you."

I take notes as he talks. But at the corners of the paper on my clipboard, I'm drawing sparkly purple dresses.

Travis raises his hand. "What if I forget the words?"

"Fake it!" I say with a laugh. "Pretend you know what you're doing."

Mr. Wood agrees. "Sassy will be backstage with a headset on. She knows all the songs and all the cues. Trust her. She knows what she's doing." He gives me a big smile. "Let's all give Sassy a big round of applause for all her hard work and organization."

Everybody claps for me. I blush a little.

"Now, costumes, everybody!" Mr. Wood calls out. "Let's do it!"

"We finally get to sing in those dresses?" Jasmine asks.

"Yes, finally," I tell her with a sigh as she and the other girls rush to change.

Carmelita sneezes again as she heads to the dressing area.

"Are you okay?" I ask her.

Her nose is red, but she nods her head yes. She can't talk because she's blowing her nose. Again.

I grab my clipboard, sling my sack across my chest, and head for backstage. Mr. Wood gives me a headset that lets me hear all the music through the earphones. It also has a small microphone so I can talk to Bill and Tony — the guys who are running the lights and sound and video equipment. It is super cool.

The rehearsal begins with the full group onstage on the risers. The song they perform is called "Save Our Earth." The tune is a little like "Twinkle, Twinkle Little Star," and it sounds really beautiful as the choir sings in three-part harmony.

"Save our earth and let it breathe.
We all can help if we believe.

Save our oceans, save our whales.
Save the polar bears and snails.
Save our earth and let it breathe.
We all can help if we believe. . . ."

The choir sounds glorious. And those purple dresses really shine under the spotlights.

Josephina and Jasmine's ocean duet is terrific.

"Next is 'Carbon Footprint,'" I whisper into the mike. "Lots of bass."

"You got it, Sassy!" says Bill from the control booth.

The audience is going to love that one.

Holly's ballet solo, which I'm watching from backstage, leaves me breathless. When she finishes, she bows to the empty auditorium, but I can see Bill and Tony clapping in the control booth. I give her a big hug when she runs backstage.

The number that Misty, Basima, and Iris sing and dance is going to be great. Kevin, Abdul, and Ricky won't have their helium balloons until tomorrow, but their song is funny just the same.

After "Let's Go Green" and "Purple Passion for Icy Blue Waters," it's time to practice the finale — "What a Wonderful World."

"Cue the video," I whisper to Tony. I love saying stuff like that!

The video comes on perfectly in the darkened auditorium. The choir sings pretty enough to get chosen for one of those TV singing competitions. Then it's time for Carmelita's solo.

She sneezes.

"I've got this," she insists.

"Take it from the top," I say to Tony and Bill, and whisper, "Gee, I love all this!"

The video begins again. The choir sings once more.

Carmelita takes a deep breath and sings loudly and clearly and perfectly.

She does not sneeze. She does not cough. Her voice is not wobbly. Everybody cheers.

They finish the song and I finally relax.

After all the costumes have been hung up and the props put away, Mr. Wood calls everybody around him. "Get some rest, my young singers and dancers. I'm so very proud of you. We are going to have a wonderful show! Remember, the show starts at seven tomorrow evening. You need to be in full costume with makeup and props by five o'clock sharp! Got it?"

"Got it!" we all say eagerly.

"So plan to stay after school. Bring all your stuff from home tomorrow morning. And two lunches. I want you to be healthy." Mr. Wood looks happy as he dismisses us.

Carmelita sneezes again as she heads out the door.

CHAPTER TWELVE

A Trip to the Mall

As we head out of the building, Jasmine does a silly little dance in the hall. "That was so much fun! I can't wait until tomorrow!" she says.

"It's different with an audience," I remind her.

"The lights will be off. We won't even know that they are there," she tells me.

"You will when they clap or laugh."

"Oh, yeah. I forgot," she says.

"It's going to be an awesome show," I say.

"So, are you okay with the stage manager job?" she asks me carefully.

"It's fun giving orders to grown men in the control booth, and I like wearing the headset. It makes me feel important. But . . ."

". . . you want to wear one of those dresses," Jasmine finishes for me.

"Yeah," I admit. "I really do."

We are quiet for a minute. "At least we get to go to the mall to look for a new dress you can wear tomorrow," she says.

I know she's trying to make me feel better.

"I do love the mall!" I say.

"Me, too," she tells me.

"And I'm glad you can go with me. You're the only one who can help me find just the right dress for the show."

"We need to find a special Sassy dress for you to wear."

"Something in purple?" I ask. "Or maybe I should find a different color!"

"Aqua," Jasmine suggests.

"Or ecru," I add.

"Sounds ugly," Jasmine comments.

"Indigo sounds pretty. Or maybe chartreuse," I say, giggling a little.

"I don't even know what that is!" she says.

"How about tangerine?" I suggest.

"Maybe azure?" Jasmine asks.

"I think that's blue," I say. "But as long as it's drop-dead pretty, I'll be happy," I tell her.

Mom's car pulls into the school driveway, and I open the back door for Jasmine. Then I gasp. "Grammy! You're here already!"

Grammy jumps out of the car and spins me around in a glorious vanilla-scented embrace. Nothing can go wrong when Grammy hugs me. Nothing.

She's wearing a long, flowing tiger print gown, and I get caught in the folds and layers. Hugging Grammy is like taking a swim in a heated pool.

Grammy gives Jasmine a big hug as well, and we scramble into the backseat. I have a million questions.

"Mom, why didn't you tell me?"

"I wanted to surprise you, Sassy."

"What a super surprise! Where's Poppy?"

"You know he's not much for shopping with the girls," Grammy says with a laugh. "He picked up Sabin and Sadora from school, and I think they're going to get ice cream."

"Will you help me pick out my dress, Grammy?"

"I'm sure you and Jasmine know exactly what you're looking for, but I'll be glad to offer my fashion advice as you try on pieces."

"How was your flight?" Jasmine asks.

"I slept the whole time, so I guess it was pretty smooth!" Grammy tells her. "When are you going to visit us, Jasmine?"

Grammy and Poppy live in Florida in a really cool beach house. Tall palm trees line the front path, and their backyard is the ocean. Awesome.

"I missed your hurricane birthday celebration," Jasmine says. "Sassy told me it was so exciting! Maybe my mom will let me visit when school gets out this summer."

"I hope so," Grammy says. "I'll see what I can do about canceling any future storms if you come."

We all laugh.

Mom pulls into a parking place. Jasmine and I hop out and race to the big glass doors of the mall. Mom and Grammy follow. Grammy walks like a queen — tall and elegant.

Grammy is wearing her Grammy Bag slung across her chest just like I wear mine. It's a bigger version of my purple Sassy Sack, only Grammy's bag is orange and gold and black and green, and is made of cloth she got on one of her many trips to Africa.

She touches my sack. "I'm so glad this was found, Sassy," she says.

"I was so scared, Grammy. I thought I'd never see it again."

"Were you worried about losing all the stuff that was in the bag?" she asks.

"Well, I had my piccolo and Mr. Wood's iPods in there, but what scared me the most about losing it was that you made it for me."

"I could have made you another," Grammy says.

I shake my head. "Nothing can replace this one. I *love* this sack," I tell her, "because it came from you."

Grammy smiles.

We stroll through the mall, peeking in windows and chattering about cute outfits.

Then Jasmine puts her hand on my arm and stops. "Look!" she says.

We are in front of one of those kiosks that are placed in the center of the main mall aisle. The sign reads THE GREEN BEAN.

"They sell vegetables?" I ask.

"No, silly. Green means it carries stuff that is eco-friendly. Mr. Wood would love this," Jasmine replies.

"Let's see what they've got," I suggest.

The kiosk has four sides. On one there is a display of organic dog food and baby food.

"I can see being careful about chemicals and additives in a baby's food, but a dog's?" Jasmine says.

"Good old Zero sure doesn't care about green products — unless they're green crayons or markers. Or maybe green Jell-O!" I say with a laugh.

The next wall has clever little home products. Filters to make sure your water is pure. Swirly lightbulbs that save energy. Reusable shopping bags.

"Look at this!" Jasmine says, picking up a really cute purse. "It's made from recycled plastic water bottles! Awesome."

"I can't believe how soft the material feels."

Mom and Grammy are also looking with interest at the purses. "I think I'll buy this one," Mom says. "It matches my new blue dress!"

"Plus, you'll save a cow from being dyed blue!" I point out. That makes Jasmine and Grammy laugh.

While Mom is paying for her purse, Jasmine and I check out the third side of the kiosk. It has organic soap and deodorant. Lotions and powders. Even lipstick and other makeup.

"Look!" I squeal. "Natural lip gloss!" I hold up a tiny pink lip gloss made from organic oils. It's packaged in an oddly shaped container.

"Guess what that package does," the saleswoman says to us.

"You eat it?" I offer.

"I wouldn't suggest that," the woman replies with a smile. "You plant it!"

"Really?"

"Yes. Remove the lip gloss and plant the package. It's filled with wildflower seeds."

"Awesome!" Jasmine says.

"Just give it a little water from time to time, and you should have sprouts in a week or so. Blooms in a few weeks."

"What kind of wildflowers?" I ask.

"It's a surprise. A wide assortment of flower seeds gets tossed into the packaging. But whatever you get will be lovely and will be unique."

"Mom! Can you get us one of these?" I ask her.

She and Grammy look at the package and nod with approval. "What a great idea!" Mom says.

I choose the pink lip gloss and Jasmine picks the orange one.

"I wonder what kinds of flowers we'll get!" she says.

"Let's plant the boxes as soon as we get home," I suggest.

"I know just where I'm going to put mine," Jasmine says. "Right outside my bedroom window."

I toss my new organic lip gloss in my Sassy Sack. I feel proud that I'm making a green contribution — even if it's very tiny.

"Now for the super Sassy special dress!" Jasmine announces.

I'm excited. We continue to stroll down the mall. We finally get to the place where Jasmine and I just know we'll find the right dress.

"Can we check out the stuff here in Babette's Boutique?" I ask.

"She has the hottest dresses!" Jasmine says with great drama in her voice.

"At the most affordable prices," Mom says. "I appreciate that."

We look around and slowly pick out seven dresses in different colors.

Mom and Grammy wait outside the fitting room while Jasmine and I go inside.

I try on the dresses. None of them are purple.

"The blue one makes you look old — like a teenager," Jasmine says. I agree.

"The green one has funny sleeves," I say.

"And the pink one has no sleeves at all!" Jasmine points out.

"This red one looks like a prom dress!" I exclaim.

I save the yellow dress for last. Soft and dainty, it shimmers with a silken overlay. I slip it on and feel like a princess.

"Wow!" Jasmine says.

"Yeah. Wow." I twirl around in the mirror.

"Let's go show your mom and grandmother," she suggests.

When I walk out, Grammy looks at me and says "Oh, yes, Sassy. That's the one!"

"It's beautiful, Sassy," Mom says. "And you look absolutely wonderful in it."

Grammy and Mom decide to split the cost of the dress. I am very thankful.

"Mr. Wood promised he'd call me from backstage so I can take a bow," I tell Jasmine. "What if he forgets?"

"I won't let him, Sassy. I promise."

As we head out of the mall, I carry my red-and-black Babette's bag with pride. A couple of girls I don't even know nod their heads and give me a thumbs-up.

"Mr. Wood said the girls get to wear a little makeup for the show," I tell Jasmine.

"Does that mean backstage girls, too?" she asks with a giggle.

"Oh, I'm sure it does. I can't possibly use my clipboard correctly without lipstick!"

We both laugh, then Jasmine asks, "Why do they call it lipstick if you can still move your lips? Shouldn't your lips be stuck?"

"You're silly."

When we get to our car, Mom gasps and says, "Oh, no!"

"What's the matter?" Grammy asks.

Mom points and shakes her head. There, locked inside on the front seat, are the keys to the car.

"How could I be so dumb?" she wails.

Jasmine and I exchange looks. That's one of those questions you'd love to answer, but you just don't dare!

"I guess I'll have to call Sampson to bring the extra keys to us. Eek! I can't believe I did that!" She pulls her cell phone out of her purse.

"You don't have to call Daddy," I tell her.

"Why not?"

I lift up my Sassy Sack, and hanging from the side is my super-sparkle key chain. On it, along with my tiny book, charms, bells, flashlights, and change purse, is a set of keys. "I have a key to your car. Daddy's, too."

"You do?"

"Remember when Daddy had lots of extra keys made — in different colors — when Sadora started driving? Well, I took a couple because they looked cool on my key chain."

Mom gives me a big squeeze. "I'm so glad you did, Sassy!"

I find the purple key, unlock the car door, and Mom retrieves her keys with a cheer.

We all pile into the car with great relief. It makes me feel good to be needed.

We sing songs all the way to Jasmine's house. Well, Grammy and Mom and Jasmine sing. I hum along as I watch the lights of the city zoom by the car window.

CHAPTER THIRTEEN

Almost Time for the Show

"Remember to turn the lights off!" I call to my family as we head out for school the next morning.

Daddy grins at me. It's usually his job to remind everybody to unplug because he pays the utility bills. "Thanks, Sassy," he says.

"We gotta keep the world green, Daddy," I tell him. "And thanks for helping me plant my lip gloss box."

"Do you know how strange that sounds?" he says with a laugh as he hands me two lunches — one extra for after school.

"How long before the seeds sprout?" I ask.

"It rained last night after you went to bed," he says. "So the seeds are nice and moist, and sprouts should pop through the soil in just a few days."

Grammy and Poppy come into the kitchen just as we

are leaving. I give them both a big hug. Sabin and Sadora do, too.

"What are you two going to do all day?" Sadora asks them.

"Listen to music. Read a book. Watch the rain fall onto the flowers," Grammy replies. "A lovely peaceful day."

"And get to know this dog of yours," Poppy adds as he gives Zero a scratch behind his ears.

"Watch out for your socks!" Sabin warns.

"And get ready to see this wonderful production," Grammy adds.

"You and Poppy are really going to love it," I tell them.

I carefully place my piccolo into my sack along with my lunches.

"I never did hear you play, Sassy," Grammy says. "We were so busy last night, and then it was too close to bedtime."

"Tonight, after the show, I'm going to give the whole family a concert. Right here in our living room. I'll even wear my new dress," I tell her.

"I can't wait," Grammy says. "For the school show tonight, and for our private performance from Sassy Simone afterward."

"You know I'll be backstage," I remind her.

"And you know I'll be proud of you no matter what," she tells me. "Now, scoot. You're going to be late!"

I grab my new yellow dress, wrapped in plastic, a bag with my dress shoes, and my Sassy Sack, which holds everything else. Cologne and clips for my hair. Even some glitter hair spray. I borrowed makeup from Sadora's room. I hope she doesn't notice.

"I'm going to stay at school, Grammy, and change my clothes there. There's a lot to do when you're running the show!"

"I promise we'll all be there on time," Grammy assures me.

"The show starts at seven. Be in your seats by six thirty."

"Yes, captain!" Poppy says, saluting me.

I wave good-bye and rush out of the house and into the car, where Mom is waiting.

"Do you have everything you need for the show?" Sadora asks as I finally sit back and put on my seat belt. I place my Sassy Sack carefully on my lap.

"Yep. I'm ready," I tell her breathlessly.

"I can't wait to see it," Sadora says.

"But when we go to see you in *your* shows, Sadora, you're usually the star! You won't even see me."

Sadora says, "None of my shows would work if we didn't have a great stage manager. We all depend on her."

"I know. But still . . ."

Sabin whispers to me then, "Don't tell him I told you, but Dad ordered flowers for you for tonight. Yellow roses."

"Really?" I whisper back. Sabin surprises me sometimes with niceness.

"We'll all be there for you, Sassy," Sadora tells me just as she gets out of the car at her school. "And you'll look great in my makeup!" She grins at me and shuts the door.

She *knew*!

My family is pretty cool.

By the time Mom drops me off at my school, I'm feeling ready for the day and excited about the night.

"See you at six thirty," I remind her. "The tickets are on the kitchen table."

"We'll be there. Break a leg, Sassy."

"I know that's what you're supposed to say to people performing onstage, but can you just say good luck to me instead?" I ask.

"Sure, sweetie. Good, good, good luck tonight," Mom replies.

I run into school, full and warm from my mother's hug.

Classes seem to take *hours*, however. In between figuring out math problems, I'm checking my clipboard and going over my notes.

I'm late to Miss Armstrong's English class because I have to stop by the music room to make sure the square balloons have been delivered. They're in place.

Since everybody in our class is in the show, Miss Armstrong announces, "Instead of doing our spelling lessons, why don't we talk about the performance?"

We all cheer.

Travis raises his hand. "Can we talk about how good we were tomorrow?"

"Don't push your luck," Miss Armstrong replies.

"It really is going to be good," Holly says. "We practiced and practiced."

"Is there dancing?" Miss Armstrong asks.

"Oh, yes!" Rusty replies. "Holly does that tippie-toe stuff, but wait till you see our stomp!"

"Stomping is dancing?" Miss Armstrong asks with a laugh.

"They're gonna be loud!" Kevin replies. "But me and Abdul and Ricky are gonna be *smooth*!" he says. "We're doing a piece about the melting ice caps."

"And we dance with square-shaped balloons that look like ice cubes!" Abdul adds.

"My, my, my," Miss Armstrong says. "I can't wait to see this extravaganza!"

"Cool word," I say quietly.

"Well, then, let's all learn to spell it," Miss Armstrong suggests.

Everybody groans and looks at me like it's my fault. But it *is* a cool word. It's like describing our show, but with sparkles.

"So what part do you play in the musical, Sassy," Miss Armstrong asks after we all write the word *extravaganza* in our vocabulary books. "You're not a singer, are you?"

I guess everybody knows I can't sing.

"I'm stage manager," I explain. "It's my job to make sure the show runs smoothly."

"You're a great choice," Miss Armstrong says. "I am certain you'll do an excellent job."

I give her a small smile.

Then she turns to Carmelita. "Are you okay, sweetie?" Miss Armstrong asks her, concern in her voice.

Carmelita has her head on her desk. She lifts it up and sniffs. Her nose is red. "I'm okay," she says. "I'm just resting up for the show. I have a solo."

Miss Armstrong says, "Well, I hope you feel better, dear. Drink some juice before you perform, okay?"

Carmelita nods and puts her head back on her desk.

This is not a good sign. I make another note on my clipboard.

Finally, the last bell of the day rings. I'm the first one in Mr. Wood's classroom. He's got on a shiny black tuxedo with a rather large purple vest like the boys are wearing.

"Wow!" I tell him. "You look, uh, different."

"Thanks, I think," he replies.

"You look great. It's just that I'm not used to seeing teachers so dressed up."

He laughs. "Everything is ready, Sassy," he says. "This show will be a success because of you. Thank you so much for all your hard work."

"It really *is* fun being in charge," I admit.

"I promise I won't forget to bring you out onstage when we take our curtain calls," Mr. Wood says. "I know that's important to you."

"Thanks," I say as I hang up my new yellow dress.

Then I start lining up props onstage, checking off jobs on my clipboard, and making sure everything needed is in place.

The other kids begin to come in, noisier than usual because of the excitement.

"Ooh, snap, Mr. Wood!" Travis says. "Dynamite outfit!"

As the rest of the class troops in, they all give shout-outs to Mr. Wood. "We should get a picture of Mr. Wood in his tux!" Misty suggests.

"Great idea!" I say. I reach into my sack, pull out a disposable camera, and snap a couple of photos. I make another note to myself to take more pictures as we are getting ready.

Carmelita, however, is quieter than the rest of the class. Instead of chattering and giggling like she usually does, she sits quietly in a chair, blowing her nose.

"You feeling all right, Carmelita?" Mr. Wood asks.

"I'm fine," she says. "Just resting my voice until tonight."

Mr. Wood hands her a juice box. "Sip this," he suggests.

She takes it, and I give her a few cough drops from my sack. I'm no doctor, but Carmelita looks sick to me. I hope she'll feel better by seven.

Mr. Wood opens a cardboard box that had been sitting on the piano. "The programs are here!" he announces with excitement. He gives one to each person in the room.

"Cool cover!" Travis says.

"I like the pictures of the water, sky, and forests," says Holly.

The words *PRINTED ON RECYCLED PAPER* appear

in large letters on the back of the program, along with more photos of the earth.

Basima flips through the booklet. "You've got everybody's picture in here! Awesome!"

"I look good," Rusty says, flexing a muscle in his arm.

"I look better!" Travis boasts.

Holly and Iris roll their eyes at the boys.

I smile quietly when I see my picture. It takes up half a page in the program and I'm not wearing that dumb old blue-and-white uniform. I'm wearing a pretty flowered outfit — with sparkles. It's my photo from picture day. Under the picture the caption says, "Sassy Simone Sanford — Super Stage Manager."

Mr. Wood sees me looking at it and gives me a thumbs-up. I grin.

"I like this section you put in the back about how everybody can help to keep our world green," Josephina comments.

"Me and Jasmine planted lip gloss boxes last night," I tell everybody.

"Huh?" Travis looks at me like I'm nuts.

"We bought some lip gloss that came in a package that could be planted."

"So what will sprout? Little tiny lip glosses?" Ricky cracks up at his own joke.

"No. Flowers. The package is full of wildflower seeds," Jasmine explains.

"Cool."

The program lists the order of the numbers in the show, the names of each of the singers and dancers, and the important "green" message in each song. Awesome.

"Okay, group. Put your programs in your backpacks for now. Let's get into costume and makeup. We have a show to put on!" Mr. Wood calls out.

By the end of class, everyone is in costume. Except me. I've been too busy to get dressed. The glory of everyone in those purple dresses and vests takes my breath away.

"On the risers, everybody," I call out. "Let me get some pictures while everyone is still fresh." I snap a couple of group shots and then take photos of the kids in trios and duets.

Rusty, Travis, and Charles mug for the camera with their shades and boots.

Kevin, Abdul, and Ricky pose with their ice-cube balloons.

I take a picture of Holly in her purple dress, then she quickly changes into her green rain forest dance costume so I can snap her in that one also.

Josephina and Jasmine look awesome with the blue cloth that will flutter like the ocean.

"Hey, Sassy," Jasmine says. "You need your picture taken, too! Go get dressed!"

I realize I'm the only one still in my uniform. "You're right!" I say. "Come help me with my makeup!"

We rush out to the bathroom.

The yellow dress seems to float onto me. I check out the mirror and grin.

"I have a bunch of Sadora's makeup," I tell Jasmine as I pull my sister's stuff out of my sack.

"She'll have a fit!"

"She's cool. She doesn't mind."

Jasmine expertly applies glittery eye makeup and shiny lipstick, then dusts my face with a light glowing powder.

I look in the mirror. "You rock, Jasmine," I tell her.

"I know. Let's do something with your hair now," Jasmine suggests.

I take a brush and comb out of my sack and hand it to her. She brushes and spins my hair across her fingers like an expert. In just a few minutes, I glance up and I'm amazed. Almost like magic, my hair looks awesome.

"Just a bit of glitter spray now," Jasmine says.

I pull it out of my bag, and she sprays just enough to make my hair glisten.

"Wow, Sassy. You look great," Jasmine tells me as she steps back.

She looks terrific in that purple dress, but I gotta admit I look pretty good, too.

We give each other a high five and head back to Mr. Wood's room.

The whole group applauds when they see me. I spin around in my dress and take a bow. It's almost as good as wearing one of those purple dresses. Almost.

Mr. Wood takes my camera and snaps a bunch of photos of me, of me and Jasmine, and of me with the whole group. I toss the camera back into my sack along with the iPods and my headset. I'm ready.

It's almost time for the bell.

"Let's practice the first song before we head to the auditorium," Mr. Wood suggests.

Everybody stomps onto the risers. It's a lot noisier than usual because instead of sneakers, most of us are wearing hard-soled dress shoes.

I set the iPod into the player, and Mr. Wood raises his baton. The room is full of silence and expectation.

"Save our earth and let it breathe.
We all can help if we believe.

Save our oceans, save our whales.
Save the polar bears and snails.
Save our earth and let it breathe.
We all can help if we believe. . . ."

It's lovely.
Then, suddenly, we hear:
THUMPA-THUMPA-THUMPA-BAM!
THUMPA-THUMPA-THUMPA-BAM!
THUMPA-THUMPA-THUMPA-BAM!

CHAPTER FOURTEEN

The Silver Secret Shines

"Noooo!" Mr. Wood screeches. "Not tonight!" But the noise continues.

THUMPA-THUMPA-THUMPA-BAM!

THUMPA-THUMPA-THUMPA-BAM!

THUMPA-THUMPA-THUMPA-BAM!

Mr. Wood in his purple-vested tuxedo heads to the door. But before he reaches it, Bike walks in.

"Looking spiffy, Mr. Wood," he comments.

"Forget spiffy!" Mr. Wood spits out. "Tonight is our show! We cannot have interruptions! You promised no more noise during the school day."

"I know. I know. I just came in to tell you that the noise will only last a few minutes. We just have to tighten up one corner. Five minutes. I promise."

THUMPA-THUMPA-THUMPA-BAM!

THUMPA-THUMPA-THUMPA-BAM!

THUMPA-THUMPA-THUMPA-BAM!

Mr. Wood looks angry.

Bike says, "I gotta admit, it's an awful racket! But that should be it. I'm even coming to see the performance!" He pulls a wrinkled ticket from his pocket.

Silence returns. We all wait for another set of bumps and thumps. But all is quiet.

Mr. Wood takes a deep breath. He offers his hand to Bike. "Enjoy the show," he says finally.

"I know I will." Bike leaves the room.

The bell signals the end of the day.

Mr. Wood looks at us and breathes deeply once more. "Let's head to the auditorium, group. Sassy, are you ready?"

My sack is slung across my chest. I pat it with confidence. "Ready!" I tell him.

Everybody is a little nervous as we run through the pieces without the lights. Misty and Iris drop the blue cloth that is supposed to look like shimmering water in Jasmine and Josephina's duet.

One of the ice-cube helium balloons gets a hole in it and sags like a melted Popsicle.

Travis forgets the words to his solo in the "Purple Passion" song — again.

And Carmelita keeps sneezing and coughing. Her voice sounds scratchy as she sings her "Wonderful World" solo.

Mr. Wood gathers us all together behind the closed curtain. We sit on the risers in expectation. "We're all a little on edge," he says, "but a crazy final practice guarantees a great show."

"Really?" Travis asks.

"Trust me," Mr. Wood tells Travis. "And I trust all of you. When those lights come on, and the music comes up, you will rock!"

Carmelita coughs a little. Mr. Wood looks at her with concern. I give her another cough drop from my sack.

I peek from the side of the curtain into the auditorium.

"People are coming in!" I tell everybody. "Lots of people!"

That makes everyone run to the curtain to see.

"None of that!" Mr. Wood warns, making everyone come back from trying to see their own family. "The audience has their job and we have ours. Places, everyone!"

Everybody goes to their sides of the stage. The choir takes their places on the risers.

I get my headset adjusted and whisper to Bill and Tony, "We're ready backstage."

"We're ready in the booth!" I hear Tony say.

The anticipation is thick. I check my clipboard once more and know we are ready to go.

Even though Mr. Wood said we shouldn't do it, I peek

out once more. I see Mom and Daddy, Grammy and Poppy, and Sadora and Sabin sitting in the third row. Great seats.

And I notice that Daddy has a small bouquet of yellow roses on his lap. That almost makes me cry.

I breathe a sigh of relief. At least Zero didn't eat the tickets!

I peek once more and notice with surprise that Mrs. Rossini is sitting a couple of rows behind my family. I also see our principal, Mrs. Bell, Miss Armstrong, and several other teachers from our school. I even notice Bike standing in the back.

It's showtime!

"Bring down the auditorium lights," I whisper to Tony. The room gets dark. I can almost feel the expectation in the audience. I sure am feeling it backstage.

"Open the curtain," I say to the curtain pullers. "Full stage lights with the sparkle filters," I say to the control booth.

"You got it, Sassy!" Tony says.

The curtain opens and Mr. Wood strides onto the stage. The choir, shimmering in their purple, stand proudly on the risers behind him.

The audience applauds, and we haven't even done anything yet.

“Welcome to our performance,” Mr. Wood says. “As you can see from the program, we call it *Kids to the Rescue*. We want to show, through music and dance and laughter, the importance of saving our planet. To show the power that each of us — especially each child — has to make a difference.”

Everyone claps again.

“Our first piece is called ‘Save Our Earth.’ Even though most of you will recognize the tune as ‘Twinkle, Twinkle, Little Star,’ the melody was actually written by Mozart in the early 1780s. Enjoy the show.”

The audience claps even more. Their hands will be tired by the time we get finished!

Mr. Wood raises his baton. The lights are perfect. The choir simply shines in all that purple sparkle.

The music begins. The choir hits the three-part harmony perfectly.

“Save our earth and let it breathe.
We all can help if we believe.
Save our oceans, save our whales.
Save the polar bears and snails.
Save our earth and let it breathe.
We all can help if we believe. . . .”

They finish all three verses of the song with a flourish. The stage lights go down, and the audience cheers and screams with approval. And it's just the first song.

Josephina and Jasmine are next.

"Blue stage lights," I remind Tony.

Iris and Misty do not drop the shimmery blue cloth. It really does look like Jasmine and Josephina are singing and dancing in ocean waves. They take their bows and the audience thunders their applause once more.

"'Carbon Footprint,'" I whisper into the headset. "Loud bass drums."

"Gotcha," Bill's voice whispers back.

Rusty, Travis, and Charles make everybody crack up with their stomp. They take way too many bows, but the audience keeps clapping and clapping.

Holly's dance solo is perfection. The stage is washed in green, and the song about the rain forest makes me want to rush to Brazil and save little green jungle frogs. She dances like a leaf in motion.

Lots more applause. Holly takes a graceful bow.

The rest of the show proceeds without a hitch. Misty, Basima, and Iris are hits with their lavender-and-purple bangles and purple extension cords.

And Kevin, Ricky, and Abdul do a great job with their

song about the melting ice caps, even with one missing ice-cube balloon. Abdul goes down the steps at the side of the stage and hands out balloons to children in the audience. Really effective.

Mr. Wood's song, "Let's Go Green," sung by the choir, makes everyone laugh again. There's a verse about light-bulbs and a verse about plastic. The audience ends up clapping to the rhythm of the chorus:

"Green, green,
Dream green,
Do your part,
And let's go green —
Or we'll get mean!"

In "Purple Passion for Icy Blue Waters," Travis remembers every single word perfectly, and he and Princess hit every note in their solos.

I am so proud.

It's time for the finale. The entire choir is in place on the risers. Carmelita stands in front of the group, holding a microphone. I notice her hand is shaking.

I hope she can hold on just a little longer.

"Cue the music," I whisper.

"Music ready," Bill responds.

"Cue the video," I say.

"Video ready," Tony answers.

"Go!" I command.

Beautiful pictures of the rain forest and the desert and the oceans fill the screen behind the singers. Green fields and colorful rainbows and lovely sunsets. The choir begins to sing again.

They sound glorious. The song continues. The images highlight the words. It's almost time for Carmelita's solo.

But she's not there.

The choir is still singing. Mr. Wood looks frantic as he directs them.

I hurriedly whisper into the mike, "Loop the music and the video. Play them again from the beginning! We're missing a soloist!"

The music and images start once more, and Mr. Wood figures out what I've done. He nods in my direction with a look of thanks.

I don't think the audience knows the difference. The piece is so pretty it's worth doing twice.

Then I notice Carmelita behind me. "I can't sing, Sassy," she croaks. "I threw up. I'm sick. I can't do it!"

"Don't worry," I tell her quickly. "Sit down over there and take a couple of deep breaths. I've got you covered."

But I really don't know what to do. And it's almost time for her solo again!

Then I have an inspiration.

I reach down into my Sassy Sack. I pull out my piccolo and snap it together in a flash. I yank off my headset.

Then, boldly, I walk out onto the stage. I can hear little gasps of surprise from the kids onstage, but they keep on singing.

I walk to center stage, put my piccolo to my lips, and just where Carmelita is to sing, I play the tune. Perfectly.

Even I'm surprised at how good it sounds.

The piece ends, and the choir takes a bow. I'm so nervous that I just stand there.

Then I hear my family crying out from the audience, "Yay, Sassy! Take a bow, Sassy!"

So I do.

Mr. Wood looks at me like I've grown two heads. But he is grinning with approval. Then he joins the applause.

The audience claps, and we bow. Again and again.

Then I remember Carmelita. I run offstage, grab her from her chair, and give her the yellow roses that Sabin brought onstage for me. The audience cheers again.

We all make sure she takes her bow as well.

She hugs me and sneezes once more.

Finally, I raise my shiny silver piccolo up high and let it take the credit.

More claps and cheers.

I decide there's nothing better than being onstage.

I can't wait until the next show.

Fifteen Ways That You Can Help Save Our Earth

1. Turn off the lights when you leave a room.

2. Unplug appliances like DVD players and cell phone chargers when they are not in use.

3. Take showers instead of baths. It saves water.

4. Adjust your thermostat. Moving it down 2 degrees in winter and up 2 degrees in summer can save a lot of energy.

5. Use energy-efficient lightbulbs.

6. Recycle all plastic and paper in your house. Do not throw it in the trash.

7. Plant a garden and learn to grow vegetables like tomatoes or green beans.

8. Plant a tree. Trees absorb huge amounts of carbon dioxide during their lifetimes.

9. Join a cleanup club in your community. If there is none, then start one.

10. Take reusable bags when you go grocery shopping.

11. Consider buying products that are better for the environment or that are made from recycled materials and have little or no packaging.

12. Support local farmers' markets. They support the community as well as the environment.

13. Write letters to community and government leaders about pollution and ecological problems in your community. They will listen.

14. Use online resources to find organizations that seek to solve larger world ecological issues like global warming or saving the rain forests. Find one that is meaningful to you and add your support.

15. Spread the word. Talk to your friends, family, and teachers. Tell them what you've learned to make your house and school as green as possible.